A Picture of Life

A Picture of Life

Roger Watters

ONION RIVER PRESS

Burlington, Vermont

The cover art was sketched by the author and painted with watercol-
ors by son, Shane, who gave it as a surprise gift to the author. One of
many visions he has given life to. Little did either of us know that it
would be used as a cover for a book.

Onion River Press
191 Bank Street
Burlington, VT 05401

ISBN: 978-1-949066-97-5

Dedication

This book is dedicated to everyone who inspired me to write. Especially to those members of the Canton Writers Group and the Burlington Writers Workshop who listened and supported me. To Rachel for her technical assistance and Elisabeth for her editorial advice to bring this book to fruition.

To Reggie who was a retired farmer, history buff and friend who was always willing to help others. He was the first to call me 'a common man's poet' because he could relate to my poetry. It's not a book of poetry this time Reggie, but I wish you were still here to share it with.

To my granddaughters Annabelle and Josie and my step-grandson Kai; I know each of you will follow your dreams, whether it is on the stage, in outer space or teaching in the classroom.

Contents

1

~

Anticipation

She was nervous and she knew it. She had tried to do the word puzzler in the newspaper and that other game with the numbers, but finally gave up. She just couldn't concentrate on anything. Why did she ever agree to do this, go out with somebody she didn't even know?

Who was she kidding? It had been almost five years since her ex-husband had remarried. She was more than ready to start dating again, but everybody who knew her also knew her ex-husband. There wasn't a thing she ever did, or thought about doing, he didn't know about.

She was desperate since nothing in that part of her life was happening. She had tried those online dating services but just wasn't comfortable with all those questions. You don't tell the truth to a complete stranger. The purpose is to meet them and feel like you have some kind of connection, isn't it?

She started to fold the laundry. Why did she ever give that guy at the hospital her phone number? They were both in the outpatient waiting room to take similar tests. He was easy to talk with and seemed nice. But if he thought the same, why did it take him almost three weeks to call her? She pondered that and decided she would ask him. That was a lie. She knew she wouldn't bring it up because she was afraid of what he'd say.

Just then Toby jumped up on the dryer scaring her half to death. How does a cat always know when you're the most vulnerable? But at least, the momentary shock got her mind off calling and cancelling. She wondered how Toby would react if she did bring someone back to the apartment. Toby had never been very receptive to men, maybe because a man was rarely in her apartment.

Toby was her act of defiance when her husband walked out the door. He took everything he wanted, including the dog. She had always wanted a cat all those years. He claimed he was allergic to them.

What if this guy is just like her ex-husband? No, no man married long enough to father three kids could do to her what her former husband did. Besides this was just a date, or was it? He had asked her to have supper with him since he would be in town anyway.

Even though she had originally said, no, he talked her into going with him. She couldn't believe she was saying "Yes" even as she was saying it. With the clothes folded, she had to keep busy doing something, so she started cleaning her bedroom.

Why her bedroom? She wasn't like that, and had no intentions, but you never know. She fancied herself as being sexy as she picked up her over utilized sweatpants and shirt. Would she even have the nerve if the opportunity did present itself? Forget about the cat.

Why was she thinking like this? No, this is fun. It made her feel like a little girl playing house, preparing to be swept off her feet as in the fairytales she loved. Well, OK, she was not a little girl in any fashion of the word anymore, but that really didn't matter. She started to sing and dance around the room with this shoe or that blouse until there was nothing left out of place, except for the perfect outfit.

She felt good about herself. With her dress chosen, the tunes continued as she took a shower. She hadn't sung like this in so long: couldn't remember the last time. She was ready with fifteen minutes to spare before her date was to arrive.

"Always late" her former husband would say. In fact, it felt as if he had just said it yesterday, but it had been almost seven years. I must not have wanted to go as bad as he did, she thought and found herself laughing out loud as Toby ran by her to the door. She had been laughing so loudly she hadn't heard the doorbell. She walked over to the door. Toby arched his back and hissed. She tried to move Toby out of the way so she could get out the door.

J. W. started commenting about the size of her guard dog. What adult went by initials as a first name? Wasn't that kind of adolescent?

As she was getting into his truck, he started talking about his. He had some kind of business with trucks, but she didn't catch the first part so when he turned to look at her as if she should answer, she mumbled something about how busy her day had been too.

"No, I asked you, how do you like my truck?"

"Oh, I don't know much about trucks. Isn't one truck about the same as any other truck?"

"About the same as every car is alike," he proclaimed.

She had never been around trucks, but it was obviously important to him, so she asked, "What kind of truck is it?" She tried really hard to make it sound as if she really wanted to know.

"Why it's a Ford-250 four-wheel drive diesel with automatic transmission and heavy-duty towing package," he proudly announced.

How in the world was she supposed to remember all of that? She could handle the Ford part but what was all that other stuff? She knew one thing; it made a lot of noise. She was trying to figure out something to say, but she didn't have to as he started talking about the benefits of diesel compared to gas and automatic compared to manual transmissions. She tried to listen, but it got to a point that she didn't care what it did or didn't do. She just wanted to talk about something she could contribute to, so she interrupted him and asked, "Where are we going to eat?"

"What?" was all he could say so she repeated herself, "Where are we going to eat?"

"Oh, I didn't think you'd be so hungry," he replied and pulled into the very next place.

"Well, I didn't mean to have you do that," she said now totally embarrassed.

"No, this is fine for me," as he shut off the truck.

Finally, there was silence. But she didn't want just a hamburger and fries. She wasn't sure what she did want, but knew it wasn't a hamburger and fries. He ordered at the register first since she wasn't ready, she finally decided on chicken salad and onion rings.

"Wow, that is some combination," he commented. "Maybe I'll try that sometime."

Why did he have to say it that way and that loudly? Did he just ask her to pick out a booth? What a date this was turning out to be! How did she get herself so ready to have such a good time only to end up at a burger joint, wearing a dress?

Why didn't he just talk about trucks when they met in the hospital waiting room, or did he? She couldn't remember; she was too shocked that a man who didn't know her was actually willing to talk to her. Did he just ask about her job? "I'm sorry, did you just ask me about my job?"

"Yes," he said. "You must have had a hard day at work since you haven't said much of anything."

"How could I," she thought. "You haven't given me an opportunity," but she heard herself say, "No, just enjoying listening I guess."

"Well, I don't mind talking so I guess we're a good fit."

Why did she say that? Could've said so many different things but didn't and now he was talking about tearing down an engine, she thought. Why would he feel she would want to hear about an engine? Did he just say rocker arm? Is he talking about furniture now? She knew about furniture but didn't know anything about trucks. Rocker arm was a stretch even to her. She wanted to ask but...

Did his leg just rub against her leg? He has got to be kidding. There he goes again, and he didn't even change the expression on his face. "Well, you ready to go back to your place. I was going to have some coffee, but I can have it at your place when we're done. Yep, some people like a cigarette, I like a good cup of coffee."

"Well, you better order the coffee and drink it here because you won't get anything at my place," she said trying hard not to lose control. "That was not why I agreed to have dinner with you, and I can't believe that you thought I would consider anything else." She didn't know whether he was serious or not, but she wanted him to know she was.

"Come on, little lady. Do you know how much this dinner cost me?" he said as he stood up. He reached into his pocket and took out the paper with her address on and laid it down.

"I have to check out the plumbing here. Don't want nothing to slow us down at your place. I'll be right back little lady."

She didn't wait for him. She got up, took five dollars from her purse and left it on the table to cover the cost of her meal. She picked up the note with her address and phone number on it and stuck it in her purse. She didn't know how she was going to get home, but it wasn't going to be with him.

When she walked out, she saw a taxi at the gas station next door and was inside before J.W. (or was it F.W.) realized she was gone. It didn't matter, she was too angry to be afraid. While the taxi driver finished fueling the car, she heard a man calling for Sue. He was walking around the parking lot calling a name that wasn't even hers. I guess I made as much of an impression on him as he did on me, she thought.

Well, at least I got my bedroom cleaned. Maybe sometime soon... She smiled to herself as the taxi pulled away.

2

∽

The Cup

The boardwalk didn't let us down. We blended right in with the cast of characters enjoying what Atlantic City had to offer, except for the casinos. I guess none of us received pleasure from watching hard-earned money disappear without some form of benefit. No matter how they disguised the gadget or the color of lights displayed.

We joined in with complete strangers we had never met and did not intend to; yet we all appeared focused on going nowhere together down the boardwalk.

Hunger finally made us select a restaurant to stop at and watch others proceed now without us. Why did people walk like that? Why had we?

After eating lunch, we accidentally found an entrance to the beach, which had been hidden by the tall sand dunes. As we topped the last dune, a beach appeared that stretched as far as the eye could see. The roar of the surf replaced the carnival-like music.

As tourists, we committed the mistake of taking our

footwear off as soon as we got to the sand. By the time the initial shock of the heat from the sand registered, we had our shoes back on with deceptive speed. We didn't take them off again until we were all but standing in water.

Initially, we thought the lack of tans would cause us to stand out yet to our surprise, we fit right in—the tourists outnumbered the locals. We were taking turns walking in the surf—flatlanders being mesmerized by the music of the waves. Much like the soft sounds of the giant wind turbines, the waves had a song all their own. The waves drowned out the noises of the human specks confined to the sand.

The search for shells in the cool water wasn't enough to hold us there, as the sun soon made us seek shelter. On the boardwalk, an ice cream shop beckoned to us, offering a famous Vermont brand of ice cream. As we were living and breathing beings, we each ordered our favorites: from Chocolate Swirl to Cherry Garcia to Rocky Road.

Dark, billowing gray clouds started to build up as we walked outside to look for a seat in the shade. This was one of the few quiet areas along the boardwalk where we could enjoy our special treats. But we were not alone.

What sounded like a squeak at first, then clearly a woman's voice, rose above the chatter of the crowd. As we began to look around, the voice gained in volume and confidence. A small, frail-looking woman—clearly a very accomplished soprano was singing a beautiful aria. Initially, most everyone seated in the area didn't know what to think. Some even got up and left the area. As time went on, many walking by had questioning looks on their faces, much like we had when she started. Many of them looked for a seat or stood off to the side to listen.

She sat there partially bent over not looking at anyone as she sang. This accomplished, elderly lady was dressed in a light blue evening gown and sparkling jewels, as if she were ready for the theatre. It was hard to believe that she was the source of such a full and distinctive voice.

We basked in her talented open-air theatre performance until the threatening weather sent us all for cover. We left with gratitude for having witnessed her performance. We—and most around us—placed money in her china coffee cup. This to express our appreciation for her unexpected gift to us.

3

≈

Controlled Dash

The small car comes to a sudden stop as close to the front door as possible. The handicap parking sign did little to deter the couple—this was an emergency. Stiff from hours of traveling, the initial awkward movements did not dissuade them in their pursuit of the entrance. As she reached the sidewalk, a good ten feet from the door, her arm was stretched out, her hand ready to grab the handle.

Once inside the building, they moved forward carefully to avoid the people looking at the racks of sunglasses and snacks. Why do they always put these things right where you come in, she wondered? As their bodies limbered up, their pace picked up and they joined in the communal rush as discreetly as possible to their respective restrooms. The "THIS SIDE TEMPORARILY CLOSED" sign diverted her to the next door. Halfway in she realized she was in the men's room. As casually as possible, she walked to the first stall: locked. She tried the next stall: locked. There was only one more stall left. She tried the door and it opened: relieved, she entered. Only a couple of men drying their hands even noticed her enter. Her husband was standing with the rest facing the wall. She couldn't believe how little privacy each person had and how it stank. When she sat down, she hoped she didn't pass gas like a foghorn. Fortunately, the person in the stall next to her flushed the toilet and left. She looked at her feet. Why didn't she wear those tennis shoes instead of these sandals? She moved her feet together, so it made it harder to see her polished toenails.

When she was done, she thought for a second about how lucky she was a stall had been open. She couldn't believe how those who'd seen her had said nothing. If a man had entered the women's restroom, everyone would have known. She smiled as she tucked her hair into her blouse— she would try to make her gender less obvious when she left. She stood there listening. She knew there were people in there, but no one was talking.

She opened the door and looked quickly before stepping out. She tried to look as if she belonged there as she moved toward the exit. Although she wanted to wash her hands, she decided not to and walked briskly out the door. She figured her husband would be looking at the snacks and she would have to find him.

Instead, he was standing at the door of the women's restroom, and she came up from behind him. His puzzled look was about to turn into a question she wasn't prepared to answer, especially there, so she turned and headed toward the exit, not giving him a chance to speak. She remembered her hair and smiled. With some slight shakes of her head, most of her hair fell out of her blouse by the time she got to the car door. Casually, she ran her hand through her hair thinking to herself as she got in, so that's what the men's rooms look like. Feeling that her husband was still focused on asking, she reached for her book and settled back. He finally pulled out of the parking area and adjusted the radio while pulling onto the highway. Silently she reflected to herself that now she understood why he's always referred to the men's room as 'the lineup.'

4

∽

Are You Ready

Ted moved his long, frail body slowly into his son Ed and wife Katie's home. They added the in-law apartment to their home several years after Jane passed. Ted was reluctant at first to sell their home and move away from the memories, but now he was glad he did. With chemo treatments affecting him like they had, he realized he would've been in one of those assisted living places by now if his family wasn't there to help.

"Good morning, Dad," Ed said from the kitchen. "Would you like a cup of coffee?"

"I would, but if I drink that we'll have to stop somewhere before we get to the hospital. I'd better not." Going to the bathroom had become an experience in itself.

Ed walked into the room and handed his father a cup that was only about a third full saying, "Here's enough to at least remind you what it tastes like," as they both laughed. "I'm a little bit behind in getting ready so I'm going to finish up," he said as he walked off down the hallway.

Ted looked around for something to read but didn't see anything close to the chair. Figures, he thought. Katie is the reader in this family. Maybe he should go back and get a book.

His attention was drawn to the TV where a person was belittling entitlements. "If they cut my Social Security and alter Medicare anymore, I don't know what I'll have to do," he thought.

When the chemo treatments started, he cancelled his cable and phone package. He had already cancelled his newspaper and magazine subscriptions. Sissy, his daughter, got upset over him disconnecting the phone. She bought him one of those cell phone gadgets where you get so many minutes during the year. It worked fine until he forgot to take it out of his pants' pocket before washing his clothes. Katie took over doing his laundry after that.

That has to be the third or fourth time they have mentioned Social Security and Medicare as costly entitlements, he thought. I worked hard and paid in a lot of money to qualify for those programs. They haven't once mentioned the entitlements corporations get through tax breaks that at one time were probably essential but now have become a way of doing business secured by well-paid lobbyists in Washington. What about the entitlements Congress has developed for themselves?

"Why is this station even on? They don't normally watch this channel. I've got to find that remote. This is ridiculous getting so upset over something this stupid. Are there people who actually believe that stuff? Do they really think we are that dumb? Maybe that is why they keep repeating it. Oh, I remember. We were watching a football game on this channel yesterday. That's why!"

"Did he just mention taxes? Why can't they tax the rich?

How can paying taxes according to what you earned stifle the economy? Why do some live the life of luxury while others working full-time for the same company live at or below the poverty line? Explain that asshole!"

"There it is—under the empty bag of potato chips." He reached down and picked up the remote. "There, now I can listen to the local news and weather."

"Rain tonight, possibly snow in the higher elevations. It's that time of year..." He froze as the music came on when this station showed the local obituaries. "Are they the lucky ones?" he asked himself as his eyes began to tear up.

"Are you ready to go?" Ed asked as he put his cap on.

"No," Ted said just a little too loudly as his voice cracked, causing his son to stop and look at him. "To the hospital—oh, I mean yes."

5

~~

Bare Inspirations

Relaxing on the balcony while on vacation, he felt the evening chill that was clearing the beach. Putting on a sweatshirt, he watched the last of the sunbathers seek shelter. Soon it would be dark, which would leave the intermittent roar of the surf uninterrupted.

Having been left behind by his travel companions due to illness, the personality of the room had become overbearing. He decided to put on more clothes and head for the beach, hoping a walk would make him feel better. After buttoning up his coat, he put on a hat and gloves. He laughed as he realized the amount of clothes, he had on was similar to what he would be wearing in Upstate New York, instead of Mexico.

By the time he reached the sidewalk, it was vacant. The beach appeared to be all but abandoned except for the fishermen to his left. The air was cold, but the salty freshness felt good. He started to walk down the beach staying just above the foam of the waves. He didn't need to get wet while looking for anything unlucky enough to have been dislodged and washed ashore.

His mind was wandering as he looked around. Here he was having paid all this money to come to Mexico, and barely being able to enjoy it. The architecture was different in this area, the ocean was a part of the home design. As darkness settled in, colorful lights he wasn't used to started to brighten up the interior of the homes. The last of the fishermen were gone. He stopped when he realized nothing looked familiar; he reluctantly turned around to go back.

The beach looked so different now. When it was light, you found yourself mesmerized by the ocean and the beach. Now your attention was drawn totally to the shoreline. He tried to find signs of the hotel complex where they were staying but could see none. His chest hurt from all the coughing, and he was about out of tissues, but the fresh air had rekindled him. He retraced his steps for a long time, without hurrying until the faint sound of the tinny music being played by the pool could finally be heard. The cheap speakers distorted the music so much that it actually sounded better from far away like this.

He took in the variety of lights that reached out from the big hotels. He wasn't ready to go in. He turned towards the ocean to take in the lights of the ships heading to—where? It didn't matter. There appeared to be no one on the beach anymore that he could see.

He walked toward the line of chairs used earlier by the sunbathers and sat down. He hadn't realized how tired he was, but he knew he wasn't ready to go back to that room. He took out a pen and opened a notebook. Soon he was writing all kinds of ideas. He found that if he turned to the left, enough light sifted out from around the pool to see to write.

The temperature had dropped more, but the wind made it feel even colder. He curled his body up to keep from shaking. He had considered bringing a blanket when he left the room, but there hadn't been a place to leave it safely. He didn't want to look stupid carrying a blanket up and down the beach. Now he regretted it.

He was in deep thought when a woman's voice suddenly asked, "What are you doing?" It surprised him so, he dropped his pen and almost the pad. He looked up but couldn't figure out where the person was. He hadn't heard anyone approaching because of the waves and he still couldn't see anyone.

She laughed when she realized his confusion. He felt foolish as he was trying to recover his pen in the dark and said, "I was writing."

As the sound from someone walking on the sand came towards him, he tried to focus in the hopes of seeing who it was. She said, "I'm sorry for scaring you. I didn't mean to. I thought I was close enough for you to see me. What do you write?"

Her outline started to take shape as he said, "Mostly poetry but, every once in a while, a short story."

"I've always wished I could write," she said casually. "But I don't seem to have enough patience or the ability to stay focused."

"My problem is just the opposite. When I get inspired, I find it hard to do anything else," he said as he turned to adjust the back of the chair. Turning towards her, he realized she was now standing right in front of him, and she was naked. Stunned he asked, "Aren't you cold?"

"This is my vacation. I usually come here later in the year when the nights are much warmer. Those who like the sun have the crowded daytime beach with all the vendors and everything else that goes with it. We who like the freedom of the night enjoy an intimate privacy. Most of the time, people walk by and don't even notice me. Like you, until I got into the light." She paused, looked around for the first time appearing hesitant then added, "Well, I guess I'd better move on."

"I was thinking about going in myself before you came. I've been sick since we got here. The room had become stifling, so I came out dressed like this. Even though I tried to prepare and dress warm, the wind's made it uncomfortable," he said.

"The lakes in the mountains are still frozen over. That's why there is such a temperature change here at night," she said, then hesitated before adding, "Maybe someday I'll read some of your inspirations. Again, I'm sorry I interrupted your train of thought." She started to walk away towards the ocean.

"You've given me an inspiration I never expected. Enjoy the freedom the night gives you," he said. Her reply was drowned out by the sound of the surf.

He was amazed by how quickly she'd disappeared, yet she had to be very close. He stared out at the darkness. Nothing. The stars were out, but there was no moon. Small blinking lights of cruise ships or freighters appeared off and on far out on the ocean.

Where did she come from? Where was she going? With high tide coming in, there wasn't much open beach left to walk on between the various condos, hotel complexes and the ocean.

He pondered their brief conversation, going over the words they'd exchanged. How many others were out there? What did they do? How did they find each other? Granted, with a moon you would be able to see outlines of each other, but not on a night like tonight. In fact, she could be standing just a few feet away. He had no way of knowing. Maybe there was someone else with her? Was it his medication or did that really happen?

He looked down the seating area. As far as he could tell, there was no one seated there. Suddenly, the freedom he had previously felt was gone. He was cold but, more importantly, embarrassed by the sudden chill he felt from being watched. He didn't even fold up his tablet as he stood up. Taking one last look in the direction she'd gone, he turned toward the sanctuary of light and said, "Guess I'm not ready to be a person of the night."

* * *

Standing there in the darkness, she kicked herself for the way she'd handled that exchange. She watched him as he stared towards the horizon. Why had she walked away? He really couldn't see her. She had wanted to know what he was writing about. What was it that had caught his attention? She turned towards the horizon trying to imagine what he saw. There were faint bobbing lights of ships as they faded across the horizon with lonely stars seemingly abandoned by the absent moon. It was a dark night.

She remembered now that as she'd been getting ready, she had first noticed him walking on the beach as if he was lost in thought. And when she had approached him, she'd considered sitting down with him even though she could sense how uncomfortable he was. If only she had—he would've relaxed once they started talking about his work, she felt sure of that.

She wanted to know more—what had caught his attention to the point she had startled him when she made herself known? She was about to go back when he got up. She waved at him when he looked her way, but he didn't respond. Instead, he turned away from the beach and walked slowly towards the lights without ever looking back.

If only she hadn't left? Now what was she going to do? She felt totally alone.

6

⌇

Fading Purpose

This was a busy time for Joseph P. Daily. He liked it that way. He checked his reflection in the mirror. "Image is so important," he said aloud, even though he was all alone. He reached for a pair of scissors to trim a couple of stray whiskers.

He had been working as an activist for over twenty years; the preparation part had become routine. Laura used to organize these events. She would notify area colleges of dates and times of meetings. The professors would supply students to fill these small-town halls while Joseph would present important environmental information for the various boards.

She was the only one who understood him. She arranged everything, but always made sure there was time for them. Sometimes when they were making love, he would think of this or that and want to write it down. She bought him a small tape recorder he could talk into, so he didn't forget his thought. That way he didn't have to look for a pen.

When Laura left, most everyone else did too. For the first few years, she would come back for important meetings. It was so great to work with her again. They would have some time, but not like it was before. She would say she had to leave when they usually would have talked about the night. Then she stopped coming altogether. He thought he'd seen her a couple of times, but she would disappear before he could talk to her. Also, she was with her kids. That would be awkward.

Now he was on his own, but that was alright. He was used to it. As the hair in his beard changed from brown to gray, the people he had worked with advocating various environmental concerns were noticeably absent. Sometimes he would see their faces in the crowd, but they weren't standing beside him like before. This was particularly hard to accept.

He had recently picketed the expansion of a local car dealership. It would add to the greenhouse gases with all the additional blacktop and new employees. He didn't include in his figures the additional customers who would come to buy new vehicles or have their vehicles serviced. Even though he had notified many of his former colleagues of this protest, nobody came to help him picket.

Joe was disappointed when the pictures of his arrest appeared on page eleven with the obituaries. The police claimed they were not limiting his First Amendment rights by arresting him. He did not agree. He had moved every time anyone at the dealership had asked him to for the last two months. This time he decided it was time to say no since they were starting to pave the last section of the new parking lot. This meant the expansion would be complete by the end of the day.

Frankly, he was tired of orating his dramatic poetic works and dancing in the dirt or mud. He was discovering that even he had limits. He had to give the business owners credit though, they had been nice enough to have someone bring him water numerous times during his educational picket. They were so interested and easy to talk to.

This wasn't his first attempt to prevent a business expansion, but it was one of his most embarrassing. The local police didn't even book him or write up an arrest report. They did nothing. They came, opened the back door of the cruiser. He walked over, posed for a picture getting into a police car and leaving. It wasn't until they stopped at a local convenience store that he realized he wasn't even handcuffed. When one of the officers went inside and came out with an ice cream bar for each of them, he was glad he could eat it freely. It was the kind he liked with lots of chocolate and nuts but didn't often buy because of the cost.

They didn't seem to be in any hurry to get back to the office. He was enjoying his ice cream bar so much he was about to ask where they were going when they pulled into his driveway. The officer he knew as Jones who also bought the ice cream asked, "Well Joe, what are you going to do for the next couple of months? You know I don't live that far from here. I could use some help splitting up some wood," and they all laughed.

"You never know what the next cause will be, but I don't think it will be your woodpile since mine needs attention too. No, you never know,"

Joseph said as he got out of the patrol car. "But you can bet it will be important."

"OK, Joe. Well, whatever it is, we'll probably see you, but don't forget the offer on the woodpile still stands," as they pulled away. It wasn't until he was almost to the house that he realized his vehicle was still at the dealership. He waved frantically at the officers who waved back as they disappeared. He wondered if they realized why he was waving. If they didn't, soon everyone would.

He called almost everyone he knew, but no one was available to give him a ride to the dealership. He finally swallowed his pride and called the dealership to see if they could return his vehicle. There was a pause when the owner explained that due to the condition of his truck, he didn't feel it was safe for one of his employees to drive it. He would send someone over to pick him up, but it may be a while since they were still paving. Joe wouldn't be able to get to it now until all of their equipment was out of the way because of where he had parked.

The editorials appeared in the local and regional papers. "Protester asked dealership for a ride after picketing place of business for two months." The press was not kind. The jokes around the local coffee shops were brutal.

* * *

When Joseph Daily pulled up to the front of the Stark Municipal Building, he was surprised there weren't more cars in the parking lot. Even though he was early, at least for him, it was important to have everyone notice when he arrived. That was a lesson he had learned from the professors. They used to send in a volunteer who would save the number of seats needed up front. That would ensure they had suitable seating. Then, just before the meeting was to start, everyone would walk in. The numbers caused those present to notice, but that hadn't happened in a long time.

He left his truck in front and walked in to find there was nobody but the local officials. The press wasn't even there.

He signed in and sat down. He knew the routine well. Alvin Altmont, the chairman for the meeting, looked up and said, "Joseph, we saw your Letter to the Editor. Is there something you would like to add tonight?"

"Of course, Mr. Altmont, but I'm surprised the press isn't here. Doesn't the paper cover your meetings anymore? I guess that doesn't matter. The reason I'm here is to bring to your attention the urgent concerns we all should have about these huge liquid manure pits that farmers are installing without any regard to our delicate environmental structure. These huge uncontrolled methane manufacturing systems are releasing unknown amounts of methane into the atmosphere and are causing ecological damage that remains undocumented." He paused to let this sink in.

"Farmers should have to put domes over these huge methane producing plants to collect the gas which then could be safely used for fuel. This is documented in many studies available on the web; your office has a copy. Some farms are using them which I hope you, as a responsible board, will force all farmers to comply with before they build a pit. If they don't agree, they should be held financially responsible for the damages they are inflicting."

"Joseph," Alvin began. "Do you remember our telephone conversations? I tried to explain several times how our community does not have a say about the size or the placement of these liquid manure pits. Do you remember that?"

"Yes. I do Alvin, but I can't understand how farmers are allowed to build these potentially environmental time bombs without the communities having a say. That doesn't make any sense. How can that be?"

"Joseph, remember how I tried to explain each time you brought in information about cancer, greenhouse gases, water pollution and related information that you needed to give this to your local federal agency dealing with agricultural matters? You have voiced frustration about this issue and the lack of local control. Just think about the people who have a home in the country who now have a liquid manure pit close to their homes, even though they're not connected in anyway with the farm that constructed it. This happened to my mother-in-law. The farmer responsible could've built it almost anywhere, but chose to put it almost across from her home so he could use her driveway to turn around in."

Alvin tried to calm himself down before continuing. This was personal, he didn't need this tonight. "Notice he didn't build the manure pit across from his own house, nor did he use the common sense to put it over the hill where the smell would have a chance to naturally dissipate. I contacted the federal agency when my mother-in-law called me as they were starting construction."

"You know what I was told? The review process had already been completed and the money issued so there wasn't anything they could do. This was before there was even a five-foot hole in the ground. There are days she can't even be in her home because of the smell. It permeates through everything and she has absolutely no recourse."

"Now who is going to buy this beautiful home that my father-in-law helped build? The home has not changed, but its value sure has. Here is another question the federal agency couldn't answer. Who pays for fresh water when the well becomes contaminated?" He rubbed his callused hand across his chin. He hadn't shaved because this was going to be a quick meeting.

"Joseph, we have really gotten off the subject as to why this meeting was called. Do you have anything to say about our tee-ball or upcoming youth baseball programs? That is why we're here tonight."

"Ah, no. Why would I have anything to say about that? Although that is important. I don't have any kids," Joseph said.

"We will talk, Joseph. Thank you for coming," Alvin said as Joseph walked out the door. He ran into the local paper's reporter as he was leaving. "Excuse me, but aren't you the reporter? Don't you want to know what I had to say tonight?"

"Yes," he said. "But I am late for the meeting. Maybe Mr. Altmont can give me a synopsis of your presentation before I leave tonight," as he turned to walk inside.

"Whatever happened to the genuine show of respect?" Joseph thought. "Whatever happened to—" Was he getting too old for this? He had never had any job other than this, which he really didn't get paid for, except sometimes cash came in from anonymous donors. What could he do if he couldn't be the environmental voice? He liked contemplating this because it usually helped him get back on track; it wasn't working tonight.

The house seemed extra dark even though the porch light was on. Alvin's point-blank response he hadn't even considered. All the hours of research on the web didn't reveal these real-life scenarios.

What had gone wrong? Why were some farmers dealing with the placement of these pits in a responsible way while others failed to take into consideration the inherent rights of other landowners? Still, they were accomplishing this legally with taxpayers' funds and the approval of those assigned to protect communities from such flagrant abuses. How can this happen when people are following the rules?

Joe opened the door of his rusted 1970 Ford pickup. It squeaked, not that it hadn't before. He just never noticed how much, so he went to find some oil to put on the hinges. He found some in the shed and carefully poured a few drops, or at least tried to, on each hinge while moving the door. It felt good to take his mind off the meeting. He also checked the barbed wire holding the rear bumper in place.

Ten minutes with Alvin tonight put a face on all of this, yet Alvin's mother-in-law was probably only one example. How many others have had their whole lives altered because of authorized irrational decisions? Maybe this could be his next cause. Maybe then he could earn back some respect in the community.

In any case he needed to rest. He had spent so much time researching and all for naught. Why wasn't this other information available? Had the world changed or was he finally catching up? People weren't buying the argument about cleaning up the earth for our children anymore. There were too many distractions that interfered with envisioning what it would be like for us in the future. It wouldn't be the victory tape he would play tonight. He was not in that kind of mood. He inserted one of his classical music tapes and turned the volume down low.

* * *

Laura had always helped him through these periods Joseph used to call "recharging." She was always there. That was when there were many people involved. Now they appeared more like healing moments since few, if any, even noticed or listened. This despite the increased preparation time on his part and additional information he always provided.

He looked around the room. Laura had tried to get him to quit before she left to have a family. That was what she wanted. She just walked away from the cause. They had remained close at first. Well, not close enough for her to stay overnight and talk. He really missed that. Almost as much as her love.

The last time he heard, she was an elementary school teacher raising three children all alone in the backwoods. His father had begged him to go to her. Laura was living the life the two of them had always dreamt about. He couldn't just drop in.

He had attempted to contact her, well not really. He had looked up her phone number on the computer. He was surprised to be able to see the house they lived in. Everything about it was exactly like they had planned, almost twenty-five years ago.

* * *

About all he was able to accomplish over the next couple of weeks was cooking for his father. The various nurses actually fed him. This was alright with him, but this also gave him a lot of time to think. He loved going for walks but hadn't felt like it, except for the last couple of days. Joseph composed a letter to Laura. He didn't know if she would agree or not, but he had decided that he needed a change. He needed to finally live for now rather than for something in the future, a future he couldn't identify anymore.

What about his Dad? What would his Dad do without his

assistance? What really was it he did now? His Dad barely knew the difference between night and day. He couldn't eat anything other than limited varieties of soup which Joseph or his nurse would prepare.

This was foolish, why was he thinking like this? He hadn't even sent the letter yet. He didn't even know how she would respond, or if she would. If she did, would she even want to see him? The bigger question was, could he be a father to children that weren't his? He mailed the letter. On the way back to the house, he decided he needed to do something positive. He would pick the site for his father's grave.

His father had always liked it over by the oak tree on the knoll. A shallow foundation of a small home was still located there. He rearranged some of the stones and stood back. He decided this would be where his father would have chosen to be buried so he started digging. He had brought the shovel to mark an area without any intentions of actually digging but here he was, almost knee deep.

He lay down alongside of the site to make sure he had made it long and wide enough. This felt good.

How would he get a heavy coffin back this far? He pondered over this as he dug. Then he stopped as if frozen. He would build a wooden coffin. Excited he decided to finish the digging tomorrow and hurried back to the shed.

There were some wide boards which had been set aside over the years. Sorting through them, he found what he thought was going to be enough lumber to construct it without having to buy any.

That night he checked on the internet for instructions for building a wooden coffin. He was surprised by how many different plans there were. Some of them were very ornate, complete with some suggestions for finishing it off inside. He hadn't thought about that. Why would you worry about that if you were dead? He could see that you may want to keep the ground water out but, the more he thought about it, he wasn't even sure that would be a requirement.

He left the computer with three potential designs in mind. They were similar. If the table saw worked, he would try and make the more ornate one. If it didn't, then he would have to use a hand saw to make his cuts. He would then choose between the two simpler designs which looked as though there was nothing more than a change in the lid design.

He stopped for the night and put on his pajamas. There was a smile on his face for the first time in a long time. It felt good to be physically active again. Although this burst of energy came with full knowledge of the end result. It was like his father was now guiding him through the final preparations, as if walking beside him. Although in reality, he lay unable to move upstairs.

When he went to shut off the light, he saw a little mint on the stand. He wasn't sure which of the nurses was bringing them in or how they knew he liked this kind in the first place. It didn't happen every day but, when it did, it was appreciated. He kept trying to remember to say thanks to whomever it was, but he always forgot in the morning.

There were times when he thought he could smell Laura, but there was no place for her to hide, except underneath the bed. One night he got up and looked but found only a tissue. He let the homemade mint candy slowly melt in his mouth as he lay back in his bed.

The next morning, he picked up the list that he had prepared before going to bed and went into the basement. The sun was just starting to rise. His first task was to find the tools. He finally headed for the shed with a hammer, saw and nails.

As soon as he got inside the dilapidated shed, he tried to turn the blade on the table saw. It wouldn't budge. He decided he could at least use the top of it as a work bench. Carefully, he selected the boards he would use for the sides and the bottom along with the ones for the lid. He stood one board up since he didn't have a tape measure to get the right length. He marked each board before starting to saw by hand. He had never done anything like this and was looking forward to it. Really, how hard could this be? Joe thought of the people he knew who actually made a living as carpenters.

Before he knew it, he was starved. Most of the morning was gone and there were still two boards to cut. He stopped shortly after starting to put on a pair of gloves, but it was already too late. A blister had developed on one of his hands. He walked into the house to fix food for his father and himself. Maybe he would work on the grave in the afternoon, relieving his arms from the sawing motion.

Was this the beginning of his new life? He felt scared yet elated. Why had it taken him so long to make this adjustment? If Laura got back to him, he was ready, but ready for what? He was a fool. Why did it take him so long to realize this? Joseph couldn't believe how empty and alone he felt. Laura had tried to explain to him several times her feelings, but he just couldn't feel it. What would he do if she had moved on? He didn't want to consider that, so he finished his crackers, rinsed out his dishes and went outside. He started toward the oak tree but remembered he needed an axe for the roots he had uncovered. After some searching, he found it.

The autumn sun felt good. He sat on the pile of dirt taking in the natural changes occurring all around him before realizing he needed to get busy. The axe made short work of the roots. Before long he was chest deep. Would this be deep enough? He would check the web, but it must be he thought as he struggled to climb out. He felt sad that the grave was almost complete.

It took him a week to construct the simple pine coffin. He placed it on the floor of the old shed and cautiously stepped inside and lay down. Was it long enough? It was, but it was tight in the width. His father had lost so much weight, the coffin should be just fine.

He had considered getting a job as a carpenter when he moved but, right now, he wasn't so sure. Between the blisters and a thumb nail that might never look normal again, he might have to consider another form of employment. He began to laugh at himself when he heard the mailman pull up.

He started to get out of the coffin when he heard the front door open. He ducked back down hoping the nurse didn't see him. He should have fixed the door of the shed. He felt foolish lying there not knowing if she had gone back in or was outside somewhere.

When he didn't hear anyone, he peeked over the edge. Perspiring and feeling pretty foolish, he climbed out of the coffin and headed for the dented, rusty mailbox. Trying not to run he walked fast. Who was there to notice anyway? Had Laura responded? She must have since they seldom received mail. The bills were handled by an attorney now.

Why did he suddenly feel so naive? He could be the one paying the bills instead of the attorney. This was the same attorney who always paid his bail, the one who used to represent him in court. That hadn't been necessary over the last few years since he represented himself far more eloquently. Court had become his essential platform to get all the abuses on the record.

There were two envelopes. Joe didn't look. He wanted to be in the right frame of mind before he allowed himself that opportunity. He finally looked at the long envelope. It was from a local university professor he knew well. He felt the other short envelope. It was very light. There was no return address. Did they still deliver letters without a return address? They obviously did since he was holding the proof in his hand. He tucked it neatly in his front pocket deciding to read it by the oak tree.

He sat down on a board he had brought out to sit on, so he didn't get the seat of his pants dirty. One of the local cats had decided to follow him. Even though he was so in touch with the earth, Joe was not an animal person. He always thought they were too demanding but, this afternoon, he actually didn't mind its company.

As he opened the letter from the University, he thought it was probably the schedule for his guest lecture series. His speaking requests had really diminished over the last five years or so. He read the letter aloud.

"Dear Mr. Joseph P. Daily: Professor Burns and I have reviewed our schedules for this fall semester. Unfortunately, neither of us has an opening in our expanded course schedules to allow time for a local environmental activist to address our classes. We have appreciated your enlightening informational sessions about the obstacles you incur as a result of addressing environmental concerns at the local level. We will keep in touch as we might have an opening in our spring session. Keep up all the important work to which you have devoted your life. Respectfully."

He turned the paper over and back before finally saying, "They didn't even sign it. They didn't even have the common courtesy to sign the letter. If that is what you want to call this back talking piece of verbiage."

The cat looked at him and cautiously approached. Slowly it brushed his leg before jumping up on the board. Joseph began to pet it, timidly at first. Before he knew it, it was on his lap. He thought about several things in the letter and reread it, but to himself this time in case someone else could hear him. The phrase "local level" hurt. There was nothing local about his efforts. He felt devastated.

He turned slowly so as not to alarm the cat and let the letter fall into the grave. In a way he felt relieved, he didn't have to regurgitate actions from the past that occurred before many of the students were even born. It hurt to think back on many of those issues and see how little of an impact he had actually made. Then the words "devoted your life" fell like a brick. I'm not dead, he thought. Yet in a way, he would be walking away from everything he knew. Or had it already walked away from him?

He remembered the other letter. Was it from Laura? He reached into his shirt pocket and carefully opened it. "CALL ME!" That was all it said. "That's it," he cried out. "Call me! What the hell does that mean?" Was it even from Laura? He stood abruptly, sending the cat to the ground. He remembered all the times she had asked, then begged him to come home with her. Why hadn't he?

The cat recovered by chasing leaves on the way back to the house until it found a field mouse. It proudly presented the dead mouse to him before he went into the house. The nurse was seated at the table when he came in. "I am sorry, I know I was out there for a long time. I lost all track of time. I'll start the soup right now," he said.

"No," she sobbed.

"You're crying! Is there something wrong? Have I done..." he started to say but she interrupted him and said, "No. Your father has passed."

Joseph stood looking at her as if he was waiting for her to complete her thought before saying, "What do you mean, your father has passed?"

Looking at him for the first time she said, "Your father is dead."

"Your father is dead," he repeated. "My father? The one who restricted Joseph from his bedroom, all because I messed up his medication?"

"I'm sorry," she started to say, but he didn't hear the rest. Even though she was in the room, he felt alone. Vulnerable for no identifiable reason, he had to call Laura.

As he walked over to the phone, the nurse was saying something about, "Coroner and did he want her to wait since it was going to be awhile before he could come?"

"No, that's alright," he found himself saying without any idea why. He dialed the phone number as if he had talked to her every day. It rang and rang before the answering machine came on and said, "We are sorry we're not available but, if you would like us to return your call, leave a message. Thank you."

"I, ah, my father," he hesitated before blurting out. "My dad is dead, and I don't know what to do, Laura. I just, well, you know. I just don't know what to..." There was a beep, then a click and then the sound of emptiness. This rambled on before the loud sound of the beeper started to blare in his ear, so he hung up. "Now what?" he said to the vacant surroundings as if the answer would find him.

He could hear his own heart speeding up its beat as if he was starting a strenuous part of a walk.

He knew that was not good. Then he remembered the part of something the nurse had mentioned, "coroner." What was a coroner coming here for? Were they coming to get his father and take him somewhere? Was it going to cost thousands to get him back? That can't happen. The bastards just keep taking from you no matter whether you're alive or dead.

He sprang up from the table and ran out the door. There wasn't much time left before it would be dark. He threw the coffin into the back of his truck, then took it out thinking he should carry it into the house. He stopped because it wouldn't make the corner of the kitchen. The coffin was not going into the house.

Why hadn't he checked this out before? He would have to bring his father to the coffin. He set the coffin on the steps and propped it against the door to help hold it open. Then he went back into the house to his father's bedroom. He usually checked in on his father every night before he went to bed. He would open the door, look in and although the room was often dark, he could make out his father's outline.

Joseph didn't know how he was going to get his father down the stairs. Then he remembered planning for this last week. He stepped back, peeled off the bed spread and carefully wrapped the sheet around his father's body to include his face. It was up to him to make sure his father was buried by the oak tree.

As he gathered his father up in his arms, he saw a line of new pictures on the nightstand. He thought of turning the light on so he could see them better, but remembered he needed to act before the coroner came so he picked up the package. That was how he had to think of this process. Surprised by how light his father was, he headed for the stairs. He tried a number of ways to carry him down the stairs, but finally lay him down. He decided to guide him headfirst down the stairs while holding his head up.

He was stunned by how easily it worked. At the bottom of the stairs, he gathered the package to take his father out of the house. Slowly he lowered his father into the coffin he had made especially for him. He wanted his father to know this and said, "Father, this is the coffin I made for you." He stood back as if it would help his father see it better.

Filled with pride he put the lid on. He got the hammer and the four nails he had specifically set aside. Once the nails were pounded in, he bent over to pick up the coffin. He couldn't lift it. He went to the truck, started it and backed up as close to the house as he could get. He still couldn't get one end on the truck.

He was sweating profusely when he heard a car pull up. Who could that be? What if it was the coroner?

Laura had driven as fast as she could. She had been coming to help the nurses three days a week. She was sure Joseph didn't know. When she pulled into the driveway, she could see the truck up by the house. "Joseph, what are you doing?"

Looking up, relieved it wasn't the coroner, he cried out, "Laura, it's Dad and I can't lift him." He then started to cry as he slumped down next to the coffin.

It was nearly half an hour later before she was able to calm him down. During that time, she thought she had heard the word coroner mentioned numerous times, but she wasn't sure how the coroner was going to steal all of his money.

Then a car pulled into the driveway casting its lights upon them. He got out and said, "Hi, I am Wayne Tooley. I received a call earlier. I'm sorry it took me so long to get here."

Joseph couldn't even respond. Laura asked, "Are you the coroner?" He said, "Yes, I am. Sorry I didn't identify myself earlier. It has been a long day. Where is Mr. Daily?"

"Here in the wooden coffin. John passed away earlier this afternoon."

"I made it for him," Joseph proudly said.

"It is very nice," the coroner said. "Can we have the lid off so I can confirm it is John Daily? That way I can complete the Death Certificate."

"You're not going to take him away?" Joseph asked.

"No. Why would I do that? I understand that his death was natural, so I just have to confirm the body is who you say it is. Then I will give you a copy of the Death Certificate so you can notify the necessary people. Now can you take the lid off?"

"I have a hammer right here. I already put some nails in, I'll pull them out." The nails came out easier than he thought they would. With the lid off, the coroner made his observation and said, "OK, Mr. Daily, you can put the lid back on," and walked away towards his car.

Mr. Tooley came back with a copy of the Death Certificate

and handed it to Joseph saying, "Here you are. That will get you started. Sorry for your loss. Again, I apologize if my being so late caused you any inconvenience."

Joseph looked at it and said, "I'll give it to our attorney. He will know who to contact." Then the coroner got in his car and left. Joseph and Laura looked back at the house for a long time.

Laura looked at Joseph and said, "Your father always wore that blue hat. It seems that we should put that in his coffin. What else?" Before they were done, they both had their arms full of his favorite clothes, shoes, false teeth and his favorite book.

They went back outside, took the lid off and arranged the items he had cherished. "Now he looks like the John Daily I knew so well, but where is the hat?" Laura asked.

"It must have fallen on the floor when I took the spread off. I'll find it." She could hear him running up the stairs. A short time later he came back carrying the hat and a baseball. Carefully they put the baseball cap on John's head with the baseball by his right hand. "Now everything looks complete. He loved the Sox. What are your plans now Joseph?"

"If there is nothing else, I guess it is time to bury him by the oak tree. I have the grave already dug. I think he will like it there," he said as he started to pound the nails in. "I hope the two of us can carry him to the truck." Together they loaded the coffin.

As they started to get in the truck, Joseph thought about how great it was to work with Laura again. The way she had held him, it felt like it did before. He started the truck and slowly they headed to the field.

"Thank you, Laura, for coming. I don't know what I would have done without you."

"I was up this way when Fern called to let me know of your call, so I just came right over." She didn't tell him that the nurse called her as she was headed home from here. That was why she made it here so fast. She didn't know what she was going to say if he hadn't called.

"Well, I'm glad you did. Here it is, isn't this a good place?" he asked.

"Yes, but for another reason. This was the tree where you first kissed me, remember? Later we talked about what we wanted to do, how many children we were going to have along with many other things. This truly is a special place. He will be at peace here," she said as they walked to the back of the truck for the coffin. They lifted it carefully and started to lower the coffin in the hole. "I should have brought some rope to help lower the coffin. I can go back," but by then they had it in the ground. Joseph hurried over to help Laura as she almost fell in.

They sat there for a moment on the board he put down to rest on when he was digging. She grabbed his hand and held it tight while snuggling up close to him. The stars were receiving no help from the moon tonight, but they were beautiful. Finally, Joseph said, "Do we say words over the coffin before or after you cover it with dirt?"

"I don't know either," she said. "Why don't we say something now?"

"What would that be?" he asked. He never really went to church much, even though his parents did.

"Well, I know what I would like to thank him for so why don't I." She stepped forward and said, "John, thank you for all of your help when I was trying to buy a house. I don't know what we would have done without you." She paused before continuing, "You were such a great grandfather to your grandchildren. You were always there when we needed someone to babysit, cut and chop wood and play ball with each of the kids. They will never forget you or your little treats. They will be here soon to tell you themselves."

"What are you talking about Laura, a wonderful grandfather to his grandchildren? What are you saying?"

She looked at him. "Didn't your father ever tell you? Didn't he ask you to come along? Why do you think those pictures were by your father's bed? I knew this day would come; I just didn't know I would be alone for so long. I was pregnant with Fern when I left. She is a sophomore in college now. Then there were times when we got together but then you'd get upset when I didn't stay overnight. Well, April is a senior and Dusty is a junior in high school. I couldn't put family on hold because of some cause. There just wasn't time for that."

"I didn't come over until they got older because of them. They loved your father and knew all about you. You have met each of them at various events over the last eight to ten years. It was hard for all of us to see the way people started treating you and how you tried to hold on to a dream."

"How could I have not noticed? I feel so foolish, so stupid, so... I can't even put it into words to describe my feelings right now. It's like I have been living in a microcosm totally lacking any sense of reality." He paused and lovingly looked at her and said, "We have three children?"

"Yes," she said quietly.

He turned to the grave, fell on his knees and wept. Laura

knelt with him and held him tight until the light started to fade on the truck. "I think the truck has run out of gas and the battery is low. I'll get a flashlight and shut off the lights."

He hadn't moved. "Do you realize," he paused as if trying to explain what was obviously painful. "I tried to make my father proud. It was all I knew. I didn't know anything else. He thought I was a fool at times. He would say, 'It doesn't matter if you're right or wrong if you're spitting into the wind.' He looked at the grave. "Father, you were right. I belonged with Laura." He paused and turned to her and said, "He kept showing me pictures of your children, but I thought they were the result of, well, someone else so I never really looked. It just never occurred to me that I could be their father."

Laura was smiling. He knew that, even though he could barely see her face. "They should be here shortly," she whispered softly. There was no reason for him to respond as she held him tight. Yet the one person who had helped them so much lay in a pine box at their feet. Why did she still love this man?

A short time later a car started up the driveway. Laura waved her flashlight towards the car slowly entering the field. The doors opened and April, Dusty and Fern got out when Fern asked, "Where is Grandpa? Sorry it took us so long. They let me off work early."

"He is here in the grave your father dug for him. He built the coffin for him out of the wood I was telling you about. I told Dusty he would be impressed with your work. Joseph, these are our children, Fern, April and Dusty."

Totally unprepared on how he should handle this Joseph started by saying "Hi" to each of them. They were the ones who initiated the hugs. He was a father. He was their father. They made him feel so proud yet scared as hell.

Then each of them said their goodbyes to their grandfather. Fern especially had a hard time. She was the one he always played catch with. She was the ballplayer. His health had started to slip by the time April and Dusty were old enough. That didn't stop him from working with them in the garden and fishing. He thought Dusty could catch fish in a mud puddle.

Before starting to fill in the grave, Laura asked Fern to move her car to light up the area. When she did Joseph said, "I know each of you. You were the ones who brought me water at the car dealership over the last several months. I've also seen each of you at several of the events."

Laura looked at him and said, "It's amazing what a hat and a bulky shirt can do to conceal your identity. The kids didn't need to think about being concealed. When your father got sick, they would visit him. Then they would go out and give you water on their way home. I was the one who came out of the house while you were testing out your work on the coffin. We all laughed so hard your father even smiled."

"So, he knew."

7

The Hunter

The long, majestic sweep of the hip roof was designed to provide extra space for hay storage while allowing the heavy snows to easily slip off. Its once proud frame stands covered with a faded red paint. The barn is empty and in disrepair like many other barns of its kind. Gone is the front door and many of the windows. Some of the siding has also fallen off, partially revealing wooden hand hewed beams that are its very framework. The animals it was constructed for haven't occupied it for years. Space in the barn was converted for storage after the stanchions were torn out. Now, even this space isn't utilized, since part of the stone foundation holding up the barn has collapsed: the natural freezing and thawing process the culprit. No one goes in there anymore, so raccoons to stray cats call it home. In the summer, birds such as barn swallows and pigeons raise their young within its decaying walls.

It could be repaired, but the owner lives several miles away and has constructed modern barns that are far more efficient. New farming practices have made old barns like this obsolete.

A striped, yellow cat steps out of the shadows and works its way to where a barn door used to be. Once it gets to the opening it stops and begins to groom itself. In no apparent hurry, the cat lies back to soak up the sunshine as it breaks temporarily free from the clouds. It stretches, looks around, no competition for the hunt today.

When the sun disappears behind the clouds, the cat rises and steps carefully out onto the snow. Making little noise, the cat walks slowly away from the barn. After moving out on a path, it turns to look behind as if it were considering going back to the barn but doesn't. It turns back toward the trail through the tall timothy grass which appears suspended in the air due to the deep snow. The cloud cover reduces the possibility of shadows disclosing his movements.

The cat suddenly freezes when it sees a small rabbit leisurely hop toward a thorn apple bush that now conceals it. Slowly, the cat begins to creep toward a clump of grass between it and the rabbit. Oblivious to the danger, the small rabbit starts nibbling on a blade of dry grass.

The cat moves slowly in a stop and go pattern. Skimming across the snow it reaches several small bushes in a line concealing the rabbit. Now, just a few feet from the rabbit, it patiently waits to move in. Its tail moves slowly as muscles prepare to attack when the cat's body is violently driven into the frozen ground.

The rabbit attempts to disappear. It's long gone when a hawk starts to rise with the cat securely held by its talons. As it gains height the cat starts to recover and tries to fight, only to find itself falling and just missing the roof of the barn. Even though the snow cushions its fall, it lies there unable to move in the deep snow.

Shortly after the cat's impact with the ground, the hawk strikes again. This time the fight is over for the hunter. Lost on a day when shadows of the hawk circling might have saved the cat's life.

8

∽

Stony

Stony was a farmer and proud of it. The farm had been in his family since the early 1860s. A concern of his was, who was going to take over? None of his children seemed interested in continuing the tradition. With the rocky foothills of the Adirondacks in the background, it was a lifestyle to be proud of. The growing season was short, but suitable for raising stock cows and calves.

It hadn't always been this way. His father used to milk cows but, as soon as Stony took over, he switched the farming operation to beef cattle. Stony was not a morning person. There was no way he was going to be anywhere he didn't have to be, especially twice a day. They also used to raise corn silage. With the spring so unpredictable and the high cost of the specialized equipment, he switched to growing and harvesting just hay. He supplemented the herd's diet with grain in the spring, well before they started calving. By only raising hay, he was able to get the crop off early while others were still trying to plant corn.

Even though he was considered a lazy farmer, he knew the success of his farm depended on producing quality feed at its peak.

As he reached into his pocket for a light, he could see one of the bulls breeding a cow. He laughed, remembering when the bulls were put with the cows. They had fought with each other when a cow came in heat, deciding which one of them was going to breed her. A cow now had to try and get a bull interested since they were so worn out. He made a mental note which bull was still active. He was going to separate all but one of the bulls from the herd next week. He would keep a bull with the herd for a month or so before selling him too. By selling the bulls early, he saved money because he didn't have to feed them. The prices for beef would still be high before bulls from other farms gutted the market. If there were some cows that didn't "stick" because of age or illness, Stony would cull them in early March. That provided capital for the purchase of the necessary grain for those that were pregnant. The young heifers he raised were more than enough to replace the cows he had to cull. This kept his herd numbers where he wanted.

Rex temporarily interrupted Stony's thoughts by rubbing up against his leg. Rex was one of his dogs that was so instrumental in protecting the calves from the coyotes. Some farmers shot the coyotes, hired people to trap them or even poisoned them but he couldn't do that. It wasn't a perfect solution, but he didn't lose as many calves to those four-legged creatures as he maybe did to the two-legged. Barney, a recluse who lived in the hollow about a mile or so away, always had one calf he raised during the summer that fed him over the winter.

Stony tried to keep his cattle away from that section of his property until he saw that Barney had a calf in his makeshift pen. He didn't know where Barney got the calf, but Stony was pretty sure it wasn't one of his since he didn't see any of his cows without a calf.

It was bad enough that Barney had helped himself for years to his other "crop," unofficially of course. There were times, he realized, that Barney also watered the "crop" when necessary during the rare dry periods. This was the source of his nickname of "Stony." At first, he was self-conscious of his handle, but he had been called that for so many years. There were people who didn't know what his real name was. He had to have his smokes, legal or not.

He grabbed a pail, flipped it over and sat down, much to the delight of Rex. Rex lay across Stony's feet to have his neck scratched. Rex had been with him a long time and bore scars of battles with the coyotes symbolizing his loyalty. Silently Stony wished he understood people as well as he did his dogs.

Why in the world wouldn't either of his daughters want to take over and continue the work he and their mother, Ivy, had started? Ivy's grave was here on the property where he also hoped to be buried.

Not that he wasn't proud of their accomplishments. Both of their daughters graduated from college and were now teachers. There was only one problem: they lived so far away. They rarely came home to even visit. Tess had two kids, a demanding husband and was taking college classes for her masters in school administration. Chloe, he hasn't seen since the day she graduated three years ago. She lives and works in Virginia with her husband who is a state trooper. They've invited him down but have made it clear he has to leave his "cigarettes" at home. That is not an option.

Suddenly he realized Rex was moving away from him with his tail wagging. He hadn't heard a car pull up let alone seen a neighbor, Wendy walk up to him.

"You must have been in deep thought," she said as she walked up and leaned against the wooden rail fence.

"I musta been," he said. "Didn't even hear ya drive up on the gravel."

"What gravel?" she questioned. "This dirt cow path has never seen gravel," she laughed.

"OK. OK. You don't need to define the difference between gravel and dirt. You're not teachin' no more."

She laughed and said, "Terry told me you got a nice buck."

"How did Terry find out?" he asked.

"What do you mean, Stony? He said he helped you gut it and drag it out to the road to get it home."

"Oh, was that who it was?"

"You mean you don't even remember?" she asked.

"Well, I was a bit excited," he said. "I sat down to have a smoke, to think how I was going to get that damn thing to the road when this guy came along."

"Sounds like you're becoming quite a hunter," she joked.

"Well, even a squirrel gets lucky now and then and finds a nut," he said laughing.

She laughed, gave him a hug and repeated, "A nut every now and then, huh. If I could only remember some of your crazy explanations."

"The truth is the damn thing would still be alive impregnating the mountainside if he hadn't woke me up. I was up in the crotch of that tree by the stream when he snorted. Then it stood there as if to say, OK, now it's your turn. I hadn't fired that rifle in probably ten years or more, so it shocked me to see it fall. All I could think of was, what am I going to do now?"

"That's when Terry came along," she said.

"Guess so," he said shaking his head.

"You still haven't told me what you were thinking of when I pulled up. Whatever it was, Rex was sure intent on what you were saying."

"It's sad when a dog understands you better than people do," he smiled. "The normal stuff, you know. What direction the leaves goin' to fall. If I should start partin' my hair down the middle or not," he said.

"Part what hair? You haven't had enough hair to comb, let alone part, for years," she laughed.

"See," he said. "You can't answer the question either," and they both laughed.

He pulled out a cigarette, lit it and handed it to her. After a long pause he said, "What is going to happen to our places when we're gone? You ever think about that? My girls are so caught up in their lives, they don't even interrupt them enough to visit, let alone have anything to do with the place."

"So that's what wave you were floating on when I drove up. How many places can you think of that have remained in the family for more than a generation or two? Not many. Look how long it took before your Dad was finally ready to step aside for you."

"I forgot that," he said. "I was damn near forty before he finally signed it over. Then when I sold the cows, he did what he could to try and stop it. He thought I was going to lose everything without that milk check. All I heard was four generations of hard work and suffering was going down the drain. Hell, he told it to everyone who would listen. He even told it to the minister in church when the minister asked the congregation if there was anyone we should pray for."

"He didn't understand what you were trying to do, Stony. He only knew the life of a dairyman. You were one of the first to make the changes. Did your father ever come back to the farm after you sold the cows?"

"No," there was a long silence before he continued, "No, he didn't. Mom came several times to see the girls, and maybe report in."

"Change can be hard to accept, especially when there is so much uncertainty," she said.

"Now the only uncertainty is who is going to follow my footprints?" he asked.

"Why is that a concern to you? When Dan died it was clear none of our kids were coming back. I don't worry about our footprints.

"What do you mean?" he asked.

"Don't you think I was worried about who was going to teach my class after I retired?" she asked.

"I thought one of my daughters was going to apply for your job. Ellie could have, but she likes teaching older students," he replied.

"Did you follow in your father's footsteps?" she asked.

"Well, no. But maybe yes. I'm a farmer just as he was, but more successful than he was since I almost doubled the size of the farm."

"Was there a lot of woodland on that farm you bought that was next to yours?" she asked.

"Yes. But I consider that farmland too, except for the ten

acres or so of swampland. I could have drained it but felt I should leave it as it was. Besides I had enough to do harvesting the timber when it was ready. That was as necessary to the health of the forest and wildlife as the hay and pasture is to the beef herd. A lot of people don't understand that. Some people mock me when I talk about how important it is to take care of the forest. It is a lifeline for the wildlife," he noted.

There was a long pause as both of them watched the cow try to get the bull's attention again before she said, "Do you know your success has caused several young men to convert their operations like you did. Do you realize you have been a mentor to them?" she asked.

"I have? No, I didn't," he said.

"Yes," she said and paused. "The nice thing about deciding the future of this farm is that you have a say as to what happens to it. I didn't. When I submitted my papers for retirement, I picked up the things I had used for years that were mine and left. Someone else I didn't even know came into my classroom. Twenty-eight years of wiping little noses, cleaning up after messes and giving them everything I possibly could to make learning fun." She started to cry.

Stony didn't know what to say. Then she finally continued by saying, "I left there with so many questions. Would they care for those children like I did? Did they have children of their own? How much experience did they have? I didn't even get the opportunity to help with the decision of who that person was going to be."

She paused and looked at him and said, "You have that opportunity. Will you decide you want to see it remain as a farm or be divided up into little subdivisions for houses? I don't think I have to worry about what you're going to decide." She turned and started to walk towards her car. "You will know before you leave, that is the difference. I didn't get that opportunity."

He was caught by surprise when she started to leave. He said shyly, "Aren't we, ah, aren't you going to come in for a little bit?"

"I came here ready to share some time with you and we did but not like I thought we would." She paused as she got into her car and lowered the window before adding, "You wore me out with your mind today. I'm afraid I wouldn't be able to stop thinking of the kids long enough to relax." She smiled before saying, "Maybe next time I come, you won't get off so easy."

9

~

Prickly Affair

The red squirrels had been digging through the leaves all morning. When they appeared bored, they'd chase each other from tree to tree and then disappear as if part of a truce. Then, about twenty minutes later, they would reappear and repeat the whole performance. At least it was giving him something to watch. Now, nothing was moving, not even the territorial blue jays.

Just like the squirrels, the North wind was finally taking a break on this cold day in November when an unusual cry rang out across the ridge. This was a sound he had never heard in the woods before. It sounded like a hoarse barn cat in heat, but much deeper. Could that have been a bobcat? He didn't know, but the clarity of it surprised him. It sounded so close. As he turned in the direction of the sound, he realized that he wasn't the only one who was surprised.

Carefully, he climbed up on a small, jagged tree stump to see better. Balancing himself with a nearby tree, he realized a deer was running right towards him. The deer stopped on the other side of the tree he was holding onto to balance himself. It was so close he could smell it.

The small stump was already hurting his foot, but he couldn't move. Several times it turned around in place, as if trying to locate the sound. It was a doe, but that didn't matter. Where he was, he couldn't have safely gotten off a shot anyway.

The doe finally stopped moving and raised its nose high in the air for a scent. He was surprised it didn't smell him. It turned so that he could clearly see the quivering muscles of its nose and tiny beads of moisture. He could have reached out and touched it. By now, there was no feeling in his foot. He had to do something soon.

Then came a series of hoarse screams from a small ravine directly behind him. The doe slowly stepped out and headed towards a small knoll in the direction opposite the sound. As the doe walked away, he wrapped both arms around the tree and squeezed it to take as much weight off the foot as possible. He stayed like that for several minutes until the doe was out of sight.

Slowly, he lowered himself to the ground. He began moving his leg and foot to try and ease the pain. Talk about feeling totally stupid, he looked around to see if anyone had witnessed this grounded monkey routine. If they had, the story would undoubtedly have a life all its own for years.

The tingling in his foot confirmed that the circulation was returning. The hoarse cries were now varied in intensity and sources. When he could finally walk, he had to know what was making those sounds. Cautiously he moved away from the tree that had been his crutch. While unshouldering his rifle he moved toward the side of the ravine, allowing the sun to be at his back. He doubted now that they were bobcats because of the number and different toned sounds. He wouldn't be looking into the sun or have the reflections from the snow limit his ability to react in identifying what was making those strange sounds.

As he peered over the edge, he saw movement by several fallen trees. There were about a half dozen porcupines lumbering around. Some had their quilled tails pointed straight up in the air while others were trying to run off potential suitors. They used the logs to climb on and off, around and even underneath as if there was an unmarked circular trail designed purposely to never leave the immediate area.

He smiled and thought, can't ever say I've seen anything like this before. Guess you could say it was just a "prickly affair."

10

☙

Little Details

Jim had chosen the wood especially for Eva. Cherry. She loved the color, smell and grain of the wood. She had told him that the wood had such a tone of warmth, she wanted it in her home. Besides the kitchen cabinets, there was a table and a hardwood floor in the living room all of cherry. That was why he chose this wood now.

The idea came from a book that showed how to make various kinds of jewelry boxes. The meticulous work paid off. He was proud of the piece. He decided to make another one for himself, which he did. When he showed the boxes to the boys, he could tell they weren't sure how to take it. Then they asked if he could build four of them.

Stunned, he thought about it for a while before asking, "Why four boxes?"

Almost in unison his sons, Stan and Jerry, replied, "So we can have ashes from each of you in our homes."

"I never thought of it like that before. But why four? Why not two? That way when we both pass our ashes can be combined with each of you getting a portion." After this discussion, he decided he needed to make a third box since there was nothing to indicate he was passing soon.

Several days after their discussion, Jerry called and said, "What a wonderful idea it was to make the boxes, Dad. Stan and I have each talked to our families who thought it could become a family tradition. No matter where we live, we would in some way always be together."

Jim remembered how suddenly this project had taken on a new dimension. He hadn't expected the boys to react the way they had. There he was, calling them "boys" again. They had children of their own and he knew he had to stop calling them that. It would be better if he called them sons. He walked into the kitchen to warm up Eva's meal. She was now eating nothing that needed to be chewed. Much like when we were babies, he thought.

Each time he was with her, he looked at her for some sign that she knew who he was. The last time she had recognized him was maybe a month ago now. He wondered if she could sometimes sense his pain in watching her decline.

It was not always like this. The changes came on so slowly at first, he had hardly noticed. The kids would come home and be shocked at how she had changed. One day, she went after some groceries and ended up several hours later at the lumber yard asking for directions home. With that, the marriage rapidly changed from a sharing relationship to a patient and caregiver.

The kids tried to help at first but, with family commitments of their own, that wasn't always possible. It wasn't like they lived next door, there were many miles that separated them. Jim tried to stay positive. "This will be temporary," he'd say totally believing she could work through this and be better tomorrow. The truth was, if she recognized who you were it became a big occasion.

Gradually, the visits by the kids declined. It soon became obvious to Jim that he needed help. He wasn't able to get things done that needed to be done because Eva was now walking off. She was looking for her cat or going to pick flowers. He even had to lock their bedroom door to keep her in the room while he slept.

The first day the aide came to their house was the first time in a long time that he had actually left the house for anything other than a doctor's appointment. Relief mixed with a feeling of failure tore at him initially, which allowed for the release of many tears before he came back into the house. This was the beginning of his own acceptance that he hadn't let her down. Accepting that he had done everything he possibly could have would help him through the coming months.

He knew the visits were hard on the kids and grandkids. She was their mother and grandmother, but he was still here! Why couldn't they see that? He finally got nerve enough to say this to his oldest son, Stan, when Stan was trying to explain why they didn't come so often. At first Stan felt hurt that his father would feel that way, but after some thought, he realized his father was right. So much effort had been focused on Eva that they were forgetting how to function normally as a family.

This was almost as significant a changing point for Jim as it was for him to accept, he needed help. Their sons came more often again with their families. They started doing things together, again. The change was also apparent in their actions around Eva. They felt comfortable being with her again, accepting who she was today.

This also aided the family in accepting the news from the doctors and nurses that her time was now near. They all knew it was going to be hard, even though she hadn't recognized any of them in months. Sometimes, Jim wondered if she was really in there. Who was it he was patiently feeding? Whose face was he wiping the food off? Then, every once in a while, she would smile. He didn't have to be told thank you, for that smile was Eva. He wasn't sure what it was for, but it was all he needed.

When it happened, the whole family was there. They hugged and cried, but it wasn't long before they began looking through old scrapbooks and reminiscing about the times Eva had been an active part of the family with her dry sense of humor. Physically she was gone, but a part of her would always be with them in the warmth of the little cherry boxes.

11

~

Look Up Before You Sit

The day was cold enough to require a light coat. At first, I wasn't going to wear one but, by the time we entered the restaurant, I was glad I did. Once inside, it was obvious it was a place that had seen better days, primarily as a bar. A young couple had cleaned it up and reopened it as a restaurant. Small metal tables with checkered plastic tablecloths dotted the main room. They ran in a line with the bar which remained the dominant feature of the room.

We walked through the main room to a smaller room in the back. The place was almost full. Since most of the diners knew my mother-in-law, they watched us walk all the way to our table. It was obvious some of them were trying to figure out which one of the girls my wife was. They then returned to their noontime discussions after we sat down. A young woman came out, asked what we would like to drink and disappeared. A short time later she brought us our drinks. She then apologized for having such a limited menu but explained they had goulash, hot turkey sandwiches with mashed potatoes and gravy, or hamburger or cheeseburger with chips, because they just ran out of fries and meatloaf. We each ordered; my mother-in-law noted that the reason she brought us there was for the home-made fries.

As we waited, talk centered around our trip and the kids. My wife and her mother were talking about an upcoming appointment when I felt something light hit the back of my head. I looked around. The table behind us was close, but not that close. Again, something fell, I looked up and saw there was a sheet of plastic hanging across the ceiling from one side of the room to the other, tapering downward toward the far wall.

That was when I felt something on my neck. I went to brush it off, but it dropped to my shoulder. It was the biggest, longest centipede I had ever seen. Before I could brush it off, it disappeared inside my coat. I opened my jacket and brushed my shirt. Nothing hit the floor. Quickly, I stood up to take the jacket off remembering there were two things that had fallen.

I shook my jacket, which interrupted the talk at the next table about the price of hogs and corn, but still nothing hit the floor. Apologizing, I sat back down. I was then mystified as to where it went. At times I could feel something crawling on me, but I could see nothing. Just as the food arrived, I saw one crawling on my wife's pants. They were so immersed in their conversation, neither of them had even noticed. I reached over, brushed it to the floor and stepped on it without either of them being aware.

The goulash smelled great, but I found myself covering my food with one hand and trying to eat with the other. It was good, but I couldn't eat it. I kept wondering, if it was like this out here what was it like in the kitchen?

After a while, the men at the table behind us got up to leave. One of them stopped, bent over and said, "Before you sit down here, you had better look up. If you're not totally underneath the plastic hanging across the ceiling, you don't sit there." He paused and said, "Damn good food though," as he walked away.

I looked up; I was sitting under the edge of the plastic, so I moved my chair closer to my wife to get totally under it. She gave me a look that asked, "What do you think you're doing?"

I smiled and said, "I'll explain later."

12

∽

What Happened

It was a cool day, but at least it wasn't raining. As we got ready to leave camp, I got the worms out of the refrigerator. My wife wasn't happy with them being in there in the first place, but worms die quickly when exposed to fluctuations in temperatures.

It was a sunny, crisp morning. We started down the dirt road toward the pond. With no wind moving the air, the smell as we drove through the pines was overwhelming. It reminded me of those air fresheners my father would put in his pickup to mask the smell of the barn. We drove past a doe and fawn who barely looked at us.

My wife came prepared with a book; she had no intention of fishing. She enjoyed going as much as I did, but for another reason. Our minds were on different planets, but it was nice to have her company. Sometimes she would laugh out loud or say, "Oh no." You knew she was enjoying herself as much as I was.

We parked and carried the gear to the dock. There were six row boats along the shore that anyone who was a member could use. This was regulated by the Adirondack Park Association. Since all six boats were there, we had the pond to ourselves.

The first boat we had used many times before, but it had a small leak. The next boat was a new aluminum boat we hadn't seen before, so we picked that one. It was surprisingly light. With anticipation, we set it in the water. I thought about how heavy my own rowboat at home was and how much easier this one would be to handle in the water.

With everything loaded and my wife seated in front, I pushed off from the dock. As we moved out of the bay, the wind blew us off course. The boat was not as easy to maneuver as I had expected it would be. In fact, I had almost no control of the boat. The waves made it worse. I briefly considered going back to the dock to get a different boat to have more control.

Rowing back towards shore got us out of the wind. It meant more work to get us to the floating bog but at least I could control it. The bog itself was only about 15' wide in some areas to over 40' wide. It was about 100' long. Birds of all kinds raised young there. Sometimes you could even see a fawn or two, but not today.

As we pulled up beside the bog, my wife was already well into her book. We took advantage of the wind to hold the boat against the floating land since we didn't have an anchor.

The fish weren't biting, but it didn't matter since the bugs weren't either. Finally, after changing the height of the bobber numerous times, I decided to move down the bog.

I wanted to have more control of the boat, so I asked my wife to sit in the rear. I held the boat stable as she moved past me and sat down in the center. I reached for the oars to move the boat when it tipped. Off balance, I saw my wife with one hand on the boat and the other disappearing into the water. I immediately followed with my upper half landing on the bog and my legs in the water. Somehow, I was able to hold on to the boat. It all happened so fast, yet it seemed like it was in slow motion as I watched my wife headed toward the water. It was like one of those aluminum sleds on a sheet of ice instead of a boat on water.

With the boat now unoccupied and half full of water, I looked at my wife neck-deep in the water and asked, "Are you alright? Are you standing or holding yourself up by the boat?"

"I'm standing on the edge of something," she said. "You?"

"My upper body is on the floating land, but so far it's holding." We took turns bailing the boat out, clearing it enough to get safely back in. I held it stable while she got in, then she did the same for me.

We looked around to make sure we had everything, especially our glasses. The worms and several lures were gone. The book had somehow landed on the floating bog near the edge and was mostly dry.

Rowing back to shore was easier because of the extra weight of the water. I looked at the bottom of the boat. There was almost no ribbing, it was all but smooth. Didn't ribbing help stabilize just about anything that floated? Was it because the bottom was so smooth that this boat was so unstable or was it the weight of the craft? Maybe it was a combination along with the waves that helped create the unexpected? Anyway, we needed to return to the dock. The water wasn't that warm, and the wind was cooling our body temperatures.

When we finally made it to the dock where we unloaded the

boat, tipped it sideways before lifting it to dump the water. We then put it away. Neither one of us had said anything. As calm as we had been during the whole experience, we both were totally spent.

Wet and muddy, we sat down on the edge of the dock, each with our separate thoughts. As many times as we had been out on this pond, this one had shaken both of us. Almost in unison we asked, "What in the hell happened?"

13

～

Tuesdays

She remembered the first time. She had known it was coming so wasn't surprised. But why now after all these years working here?

The flowers left by her purse conveniently out in the open, but close enough to the door where he could say that they were for his wife. She knew better. Still, a rush went through her when he walked by her door. She turned, but he didn't enter. Finally, he came in. "Do we have any more deliveries for tomorrow?" he asked. "No," she replied and then added, "Thank you for the flowers, Frank." "Oh, well, you know," he stammered. He was about to continue when she said, "They are nice, but I don't think I'll be taking them home. I'll leave them in the office if that's alright." "Oh, that is fine. I didn't think about that," he said and nervously backed out of the office. She cleared a place by her phone and set them down.

What would it be like, she thought? He had such a reputation, but this was foolish to even think about. Time to go home, yet she caught herself checking his office. He was in the garage with the men having a beer.

He looked around. There were half as many drivers as there used to be because of all the changes on cross border shipping. This caused a number of companies on both sides of the border to close or move. This meant there was reduced need for regional trucking services. You had to go big or get out. He wondered what was next as he saw the last of the men pull out of the parking lot for Toni's Bar and Grill. It would have been nice to see who was dancing tonight but he was beat. He finished his beer, then shut the shop lights off. He opened the door to go to his office and was stunned to see Jessica still there. "You're still here," he said.

"Yes, I am," she said quietly and walked over to him. She touched his arm and said, "Follow me home," then walked out the door.

Was it the beer or did she really say, "Follow me home?" He reached for his keys to lock up as she was pulling out of the parking lot. He tried the lock, but it didn't fit. He looked at his keys and realized he had the truck keys. He finally found the right keys, locked up and almost ran to his car.

Slow down you fool. Somebody might be watching. Don't need to have people asking him embarrassing questions. At least, not about something he didn't want everyone to know. But then, what was there to know about, he thought as he pulled onto the road.

Jessica had worked for him in sales until she and Dan had children. She then took the bookkeeping job for less money but liked it so well she stayed with it even though the kids were now in school.

What was he doing, he thought as he drove into her driveway? He pulled in back of the house so his truck wouldn't be visible, got out and stumbled toward the door. Get a hold of yourself, he thought. You only had a few beers, and she probably just wants you to pick something up.

That thought changed as she opened the door. What she was wearing was not what she had on at work. "Are the..." was all he had a chance to say before she interrupted him and said, "The kids are at my mother's, and Dan always works late on Tuesday night." She took his hand and lead him to the bedroom door.

"I've never done this before, so I don't know what to do, but I know we don't have a lot of time, so I hope the message is clear," she whispered as she nervously turned hoping his lips weren't too far away. He was caught by such surprise at how quickly she was on him that he regretted having had that last beer. He wanted to tell her that maybe another time would be better, but his response to her left little doubt he was ready.

* * *

As they dressed, he didn't know what to say. It happened so fast. He didn't want to make any excuses, but thought maybe he should say something when she asked, "Next Tuesday?" "That would be great," he stammered as he headed for the door.

He got in his truck and noticed he had forgotten to zip up his pants. He tried to think if he'd forgotten anything else as he pulled out of the driveway.

Instead of driving home, he turned toward the shop. He needed to think before he went home. She was not like any of the others. She was respected by everyone. Nobody would ever believe it. That's why this was so different.

He sat in the parking lot for a while thinking about what had happened and how it had unfolded. One thing was for sure, he wouldn't waste time with the boys next week. As he stared ahead, he noticed the light his wife had wanted fixed by the sign. He decided he would have Sunny fix it in the morning and he started home.

Well, he started that way, but turned toward Jessica's house. Dan was home now. With all the lights on the kids must be home too. A few minutes later, he pulled into his own driveway and pushed the button for the garage door opener by habit even though he knew it didn't work. He hadn't changed the battery in the remote. He mumbled to himself that would be something else he would have Sunny fix tomorrow.

As he walked in the door, Suzie and Tim were waiting for him, each talking about what they had done at school, neither willing to let the other go first. Was this what it was like when he was growing up with his sisters he thought? He quickly grew impatient and interrupted them, "Suzie, you can tell me about your book. Tim, you can show me your new project after we eat."

That brought about the response he expected, "I told you so," taunted Suzie.

"That's what you said last night, and you didn't have time Dad. Why does she always get her way?" Tim asked, as he stomped off.

"That's enough young man!" Ann said. "Your father has worked all day. Why do we always have to go through this? Suzie, finish setting the table before you get your book." She turned to Frank, "Do you want water or iced tea while you're relaxing?"

"Water would be fine," he said as he bent over to take off his shoes. "Tim, where are my slippers?" he demanded. "That kid is always running off with my slippers. Why, Ann?" he whined, not really expecting an answer.

"Tim likes to be like you. You know that. He can't wait until he can ride with you in the truck making deliveries and helping you. He takes off his shoes, puts your slippers on and stumbles all over the house." Ann turned and yelled around the corner, "Tim, your father needs his slippers," then sets down his glass of water before heading back to the stove.

"We got another bill from the parts dealer today," she said. "Why are they sending them here? I thought you said you had paid them. It says we are over 120 days late."

"Don't start with me on that." Frank said. "I don't know why they are sending the bill here. I'll call them in the morning."

She started to say, "But why?" but he cut her off. "Ann, I told you and I don't want to have to tell you again."

She turned away trying to hide the tears, in case they came. Her arm and side still hurt from the other night when she had crossed the line. It had been almost a week since he had hit her, but each time, it reminded her of the abuse her own mother had taken. She had sworn it would never happen to her, yet here she was. Deep in thought, she realized he was yelling at her, something about 6 o'clock.

"You know woman, when you took that job, you said you would have the supper on the table by 6 p.m. It is now 6:03

and I don't see anything in the way of food on this table." He slammed it with his fist.

She grabbed a fork and took one pork chop out of the pan, put a potato and some corn on a plate and set it in front of him, expecting to get hit. She turned away to reduce the blow only to realize he was looking out the window. She was almost to the stove when she heard the metal click of the silverware. Nobody else came... the kids knew to stay away. He sat there and ate all alone while she tried to look like she was busy with some dishes.

Well, at least he was able to eat in peace he thought as he finished up. He needed to go to the shed and check on the horses. Now was as good a time as any. Maybe then the kids would be in bed and he could watch TV. He got up without saying a word, put his shoes back on and walked out the door.

His behavior was becoming a family pattern. Just what she had not wanted. The kids came in and sat down. Tim looked at her, "What did you do wrong this time?" while Suzie was mumbling something about how she had to turn in her book in the morning. "Maybe he'll finish up early and see it before I go to bed," she said.

"Maybe!" her mother said. "Don't count on it though. You know, he usually doesn't come back in until you're both in bed." There was nothing else said while they ate. "There is some chocolate cake left. Who would like some?" she asked receiving an instant, "I do," from both kids.

After finishing the dishes, she went to check on the kids. As she walked by the window, she could see the barn lights were still on. He's going to wait until its bedtime, she thought. With Tim starting high school next year, and then Suzie right behind him, she wondered why Frank treated his kids the way he did.

Tim really needed his father. Frank just couldn't see that. What really hurt her was when Tim would ask, "What did you do now?" Tim must really believe that she was to blame.

As she got to the stairs, she stopped, sat down and just cried. She hadn't done that in a longtime. Was it the pain in her side from the injuries or her embarrassment? She slowly gathered herself, then went into the bathroom to wash her face before going upstairs to check on the kids about their homework.

Both were very good students. That was one thing Frank did seem to care about. Both of the kids had stopped playing sports because he was too busy to take them, pick them up or even go to any of their games. He did give them money when they got good grades though. Well, sort of. He would ask her for the money in private. Then he would make a big deal about giving it to them without ever mentioning her. The kids didn't have a clue as to what he'd done.

"Bedtime my wonderful children. Don't forget to brush your teeth," she said. "Does anyone need anything special for this week? I'm going to the grocery store tomorrow."

"Don't be late, Mom!" Tim implored. "I really want to show Dad my project tomorrow. I have to turn it in soon."

"OK," she said. "Would you like pizza?"

"No, Mom," Suzie answered. "Dad doesn't like pizza."

"OK, chicken it is then. Good night now." she said as they each turned out their lights. "Love you," she said. "Don't be late, Mom," Tim repeated.

As she headed toward her room, she knew it would be another night alone. She turned on the TV, tried several different channels, then decided to read. She vaguely heard Frank go into the basement before she fell asleep.

* * *

The week had gone by so fast. He had borrowed money from his oldest sister to pay his bills. This was becoming a common practice, but she never denied him. He always promised to pay her back, but she knew he wouldn't. Her husband, Jack, would never miss it, and besides, he was always wanting her to get out and do things. Of course, she didn't dare tell him what she really did with her money.

With the bills current, Frank could afford to splurge a little on a few of his friends. It was almost always chocolate. Just enough to know he had spent some money on them, but not too much so they didn't consume all the evidence.

You had to always be thinking and F. L. was always doing that. That was what he liked to be called. Few people called him Frank except his wife. She refused to call him F. L. even though he had told her to. She knew as well as he did all the words that F and L could be linked to, which was why she refused. He didn't care. He thought it sounded important. Anyone else's opinion didn't really matter anyhow.

It was now Monday and Jessica hadn't even mentioned it. Almost a whole week had gone by and she hadn't given him a knowing smile or anything. She did replace the flowers he had given her with some she had brought from home. He noticed how she had walked through the shop so everyone could see her bringing them in.

He wanted to ask her if they were still on for Tuesday but found himself already making an excuse to the others that he wouldn't be having the usual beer with them tomorrow. They didn't even seem to care as they started making plans to get together at a nearby fishing hole. By the time they left, each knew what they were going to bring for the cookout.

So much for them missing him. He went into his office to get his truck keys and there, on his phone was a note with one word that said, "Tuesday."

He could remember little from the first time but remembered volumes over the next months. Every Tuesday, he put up a sign she had made by his phone. If it was still there when he got ready to leave, it was clear to come over. If it was in his desk drawer, it was not.

The company was changing focus. The staff had set up a greenhouse that a customer couldn't afford the shipping fees for. He rented it out for two years. He was surprised how it took off, so he then took it over, well, with the help of his sister. There was almost as much greenhouse equipment in the garages now as there were trucks.

He had several home deliveries to make now that he wouldn't have had before. He knew it was because of Jessica. She had made him a better lover. He wouldn't admit that to anyone, of course. There were things others were allowing him to do that they would have never allowed before. He enjoyed it. He was finally good at something.

* * *

Tim and Suzie had convinced him to expand the greenhouse since they could now help. That brought people in the door he had never seen looking for vegetable plants and flowers. They had a few trees to offer, but he didn't like having trees, they were too permanent and took up too much space. Flowering shrubs were fine since they seemed to increase the number of deliveries which Tim was starting to make also.

While Frank's life seemed to prosper, Ann's seemed to dissipate with the loss of the company of her kids. They were either at a friend's house or at the greenhouses. Their friends never came over, so she wasn't even able to get to know who they were. She really missed that. Now she was really alone. Her job just wasn't enough. Her life was becoming sterile.

She tried different activities at church. That worked for a while only to find that there were a lot of other people whose lives weren't what they appeared to be and that made her feel uncomfortable. She then tried a quilting class. She got pretty good at the sewing but had trouble with the pattern combinations. She needed something more like those paint-by-number kits, but for quilters.

When she completed her first quilt, she laid it out on the sofa to check it when Suzie came in. It was one of the few times that her daughter had ever praised her for doing anything other than cooking. Suzie wanted to know all about it, so Ann explained how she made it. Later she made two more of them almost identical, putting one in Suzie's hope chest and setting another aside for Tim, if and when he got married. He was, after all, developing quite a reputation, despite her efforts.

Suzie tried to learn quilting too but gave it up after only a few tries. Putting the patterns together wasn't something she was good at. She also didn't like all the sitting and isolation. In the greenhouse, you never knew who was going to come in or for what. She enjoyed helping people.

The original quilt laid on the sofa for over two years before F. L. noticed it. If it hadn't been for his oldest sister, Mary being there, he probably would have never seen it since he didn't go to that part of the house anymore. Mary was gushing about it, asking about the classes and who came. All Frank said was, "How much did this cost me?" as if it were coming out of his pocket, when in fact he didn't even pay for any of the household expenses anymore. If it hadn't been for Mary, they wouldn't even have a vacation. Mary paid for them to come to New Mexico for two weeks every winter. Whether Frank realized it or not, this was a fringe benefit for Ann staying married to him.

* * *

Things started to get complicated for Jessica as her kids got older. They didn't want to stay at her mothers on Tuesday anymore. Now what was she going to do? Ben wanted to join the jazz band. He loved to play the drums. Larry wasn't sure what he wanted to do but "it was so boring at Gram's." He was the athletic one, always kicking or throwing something around. Drum lessons led to the formation of a band for Ben and various sports for Larry allowed most Tuesdays to continue to be hers.

She was going through changes herself, especially physically. This time with F.L. had become important to her. She didn't even think of it as wrong anymore. With the kids now involved in their activities, she could set the time around their schedules.

She didn't know why she felt comfortable asking Frank to do things to her she would never ask Dan to do. If it felt good, they would continue. If it didn't, they would stop. Many times, she wondered why she couldn't be as open with Dan? Why was it that she could experiment so freely with Frank and not her own husband? Was it that she felt Dan wouldn't be open to such changes, or was it he would question where she had heard or even learned about such things? That bothered her. Her love for Dan was stronger now than it had ever been. He was such a great father and husband. He was always there to support her and the kids. Why did she need Frank?

* * *

The business had added two more greenhouses at Tim's urging, built with Mary's money. Because of this, F. L. hardly recognized his business. They had also started contracting to do landscaping, an idea Tim had brought back from one of their visits to New Mexico. He was turning into quite a businessman and taking chances F. L. never would have. Between Tim organizing and hiring part-time people and Jessica handling the bookkeeping and scheduling, his responsibilities had diminished to a few special deliveries. It bothered him that Jessica knew this. Somehow, that hadn't changed Tuesdays.

Suzie had started college classes in Albany. Then shortly before Ann retired, Suzie found out she was pregnant. When her boyfriend discovered this, he left. That was when Ann moved to Albany to help Suzie so she could continue her classes.

Must be a woman thing F. L. thought, he hadn't even seen the little bastard. There was no reason to go all the way to Albany if Ann was there. He didn't have to see or hear from her. But now he had to pay the household expenses. Damn, that was adding up to be quite a bit. It cut into his play money and here Tim was talking about replacing the van. Jessica claimed the money was already set aside for the new van and a new tractor. "Tractor? What do we need a tractor for? We sell flowers," he had protested.

"For landscaping," Tim and Jessica had said almost in unison. "Handling the trees and shrubs would be so much easier," Tim replied. "We could handle bigger trees in the bucket. There's a big demand in that area, Dad. We now have to let it go or hire extra help just to try and move them. It would actually save us money."

F.L. supposed he could see what Tim was talking about. New homes were going up around the lake. People were retiring, moving into the area buying land and building homes which no locals could afford. If they could get some of those people as customers, it would be easy money for the business, and ultimately, for him.

* * *

Jessica sat on the hard bleachers watching Larry play soccer. She enjoyed his games, no matter what he was playing, but this was Tuesday. She had had to cancel tonight because of it. The game ended; his team had won. She was standing there waiting for him when one of Dan's coworkers came towards her. She couldn't remember her name and felt foolish when all she could say was "Hi." His coworker didn't bail her out either but asked about Jessica's husband. "Where is Dan? I thought for sure I'd see him here tonight."

"Oh, it's Tuesday." Jessica replied. "He always works late on Tuesday."

Dan's coworker looked at her with a stunned expression and finally said, "Dan hasn't worked late on Tuesday for about five or six years."

The look on Jessica's face had to have been easy to read as

she sat back down on the bleacher. The coworker said something like, "Too bad Dan missed the game," and walked away.

He knows. That was all she could think of. He knows. She could not even put her current feelings into words. He knows. She sat there totally incoherent as to what was going on around her. Somebody had touched her arm. She finally realized it was her son asking her, "Mom, are you alright?"

* * *

Dan had stayed longer than he should have. He had wanted to be in the stands but instead watched the game from the parking lot. This was a big game; he knew where he would be Friday. He pulled out before he could be seen leaving but headed in the opposite direction of home, more by habit now than anything.

He had fixed up the old shed that used to be a sugar shack, but he didn't want to be alone. He went to the next town and stopped at a place that had a bar on one side and a restaurant on the other side in a separate room. The restaurant was empty, but the bar was full. He ordered an iced tea and was about to take a sip, when he heard the guys next to him talking about F. L. He looked in the direction they were looking and there he was with a woman close to half his age and by their conversation, married to one of their friends. It wasn't Dan's wife, but he knew as he looked at his watch it could've been because of the time and the fact it was Tuesday.

F. L. wouldn't have pants to put on if it hadn't been for his sister and his son. Fucking Loser, that's what most people called him. Privately, Dan called him "Fat Leroy" because of the way his ass had looked in the window that day, years ago. Dan had seen Frank's truck when he pulled in to surprise his wife about not having to work late anymore on Tuesdays. He would have walked right in on them if the bedroom window hadn't been open. He heard noises and looked in before entering the house. The surprise was on him. How long had this been going on? He couldn't believe Jessica would do this to him. Somehow, he'd gathered the strength to leave without confronting the two of them.

A friend at work, the next day realized something was wrong. At first, he couldn't talk about it. Then when he did, to his surprise the guy just listened. He felt better being able to talk to someone about it. Finally, the guy asked, "Do you have a night of the week that is just yours where you go bowling, play softball or anything like that?"

He didn't but it took him a while to say, "No!"

"I can't imagine what it could be like or what I would do if that happened to me. I have to give you a lot of credit for the way you have handled this so far. From what you have said, nothing else has changed. How can you use this time for yourself? Something you have always wanted to do?" He stopped, shook his head as he sat down.

"I'll have to think about that," Dan said. He had always wanted to learn to carve, but where? I have an old shed I could fix up, he thought, but said, "I see what you're saying, but it doesn't make it easier when you know what's going on."

"I understand that," the guy said. "But you're going to do something stupid if you don't put this energy to a positive use."

He was right and Dan knew it. So, he fixed up the roof of the shed first and then the doors to keep the critters out. Over time, he developed the shack into quite a workshop and was getting pretty good at wood carvings, if he did say so himself.

Tonight, in the bar, as he turned to leave, he wondered if he would give the same advice to the husband of the woman Fat Leroy was with tonight? He didn't think so. This was such a public exhibition; he was thankful Frank didn't lower Jessica or himself with this type of spectacle. He checked his watch. It was safe now to go home. He was glad Fat Leroy hadn't seen him.

* * *

Jessica tried to stand but she couldn't and asked Larry to sit down. "Who do you play next?"

"We don't know yet Mom. Are you sure you're alright?" he asked her again. After a moment's hesitation, looked up, "I hope so." From the look on her face, Larry was able to tell that something was wrong. She sighed, "Let's go home. Would you like to drive?"

He had just gotten his Learner's Permit. He all but burst off the bleachers. "Of course, I'd like to drive," he exclaimed, and reached down to help her.

* * *

They were all home when he pulled in. Dan decided to put the car in the garage though he didn't know why. Maybe it was to give him more time to prepare. Maybe he just needed more time to put away his thoughts arising from the scene in the bar. As he walked toward the house, he couldn't help but noticing the flowers. Jessica always did such a great job with them. He had felt it was her way of extending the picture frame of their home. It was so inviting. As he got to the door, he took one last look and wondered, was this the way Fat Leroy came in or was it through the back door? He decided that he didn't really want to know. By this time, it wasn't even important.

As he entered, Larry was talking on the phone. Jessica was not in the room. "Hi, Son. How was the game?"

"A tough one, Dad. We won 2 to 1. We play Friday. Can you make it?" he asked.

"You bet I can, Son. Where's your mother?" he asked.

"She's laying down. She didn't look so good after the game; said she'll feel better later."

"I'll check on her," Dan and headed toward their bedroom.

He peeked through the partially closed door. It looked like she was asleep, so he went back to the kitchen. Larry was talking on the phone again but this time it was with Ben. They were so different, but yet seemed to be able to talk about anything. Ben was in college now and his band was doing really well. His girlfriend was now one of the singers plus she played bass guitar. He seemed happy and Dan was so proud of what he had accomplished.

He started to run water for some coffee and got out a couple of cups for himself and Larry. He wondered if there were any cookies left and got them out. As he sat down, he remembered the ice cream. Why not he thought, special occasion like this. Larry had one more year before he would be following in Ben's footsteps and be off to college. He wanted to get into sports medicine and become an umpire, he loved outdoor sports. Dan knew he would be good at whatever he decided to do.

Larry finished talking with his brother and sat down to help him finish the ice cream and cookies. He was talking so much about the game they forgot the coffee. Eventually he got up and said, "Well, Dad, I've got some English to finish up. I'll see you in the morning," and off he went.

"Goodnight, Son." Dan said as he picked up the dishes and rinsed them out. He noticed the coffee, but decided it was too late and would save it for the morning.

He checked the weather for tomorrow. He didn't know why, must be one of those things you learn growing up on a farm that just stays with you. He took his time in the bathroom. By the time he got out, Jessica had changed clothes and was asleep.

* * *

When he got up the next morning, he got ready and then went to the kitchen to warm up last night's coffee. He could hear Jessica now in the bathroom. "Feeling better?" he asked. "Yes, thank you," she replied.

"There's hot coffee. I'm going to meet a possible new shipping firm first thing this morning, so I have to leave early. Have a good day," he said as he headed out the door.

Alone now, Jessica looked into the mirror, "He didn't say anything. What kind of a man does that?" she cried out. Almost without thinking she replied, "A man that loves you!" and cried. To think of the things she had done, even if it was for only a few hours each week, it was done with someone she had used who was basically faceless to her. She suddenly wanted to be with someone who meant something to her, but he had just walked out the door.

She finished getting ready for work early, got the coffee Dan had left and walked out to the car. She looked around her; she loved this place. Could she remove the stain? She would start this morning she resolved.

When she got to work, she prepared a note that said, "No More Tuesdays," and walked to his office. A bra lay on the floor by his desk. The desk lamp was also on the floor. She opened the top drawer, removed her previous sign and crumpled it with the one she had in her hand. There was no need to say anything. The evidence of her replacement was everywhere.

She left Frank's office and was on her way to hers when Tim walked in. He had fallen in love and it showed. He gave Jessica the receipts from the day. They had just completed a big landscaping job and were about to start another. Business had never been better. Everything was paid off; money was set aside for next spring's orders and taxes. Tim was a good businessman. Together, they had cleverly put funds into different accounts, so F. L. didn't have a clue how much they had. Better yet, he couldn't get at the money. They kept enough in his personal account to keep him happy.

* * *

It was now Friday, game day. Dan and Jessica were in their usual place. So much had happened, yet so little. F. L. hadn't even come into work all week, which was unusual, even for him. His office was as he had left it. She checked the bra and knew Tim had also. He said, "It belonged to someone who sports a pair of 34 Bs, she must not need it."

Dan had still said nothing. Nothing had changed as she had imagined it would. They had even parted the sheets pretty effectively. She wanted to ask him to do some different things, but she knew it wasn't time to cross that bridge yet. She had to find out what he had been doing on Tuesdays after work. Was he seeing someone? She couldn't blame him if he was.

The game was about to go into overtime when there was a breakaway and the other team scored. The season was over. Everyone applauded the players on both teams because it had been a great game.

After they got home, Larry left for a team party. Jessica asked Dan, "Would you like to take a walk?"

"Where would you like to go?" he asked.

"How about down the old lane to the sugar shack. I haven't been back there in years."

"OK," he said. "Let me change my shoes," and he went into the bedroom.

Jessica had packed some water and fruit. When they got to the drive, she was surprised to see there had been recent travel down the lane. "Why would somebody be using our lane?" she asked.

"Maybe Larry and his friends. Who knows? Sometimes I come down here myself," he admitted.

"Oh, I didn't know that," she said. She had been trying to figure out how to tell him, how to convince him that it would never happen again, but she hadn't found the words yet. Instead, they talked about the wildflowers and the birds. Before they knew it, they were coming up to the building.

As soon as she saw it, she knew where most of his Tuesdays had been spent. It was beautiful how he had restored the old building. She asked him all about it, when he had made the repairs and who had helped. Why hadn't he told her?

She didn't mean to ask the last question because she already knew the answer but fortunately, he didn't try to answer. "Can we go inside?" she asked. He was not prepared for that. He worried she would ask a lot of questions. He didn't know if he could be honest and tell her. He looked at her and calmly said, "The door is unlocked."

"Does that mean yes?" she asked again. He finally said, "Yes," but didn't want to, that space was his. The thought of her entering it made his knees weak. Why? No. He knew why. But if it hadn't happened, none of this would have.

She walked up to him. Gave him a long knowing kiss then turned toward the door with his hand in hers. She could sense this was difficult for him and knew why. As she opened the door, she realized where those beautiful flower ornaments and picture frames had come from that he said he'd bought over the years. Dan had carefully created them. He hadn't bought them as he had claimed.

She pulled on his hand as she walked in, stunned at the variety of completed pieces she was looking at. He tried to stay out. He wasn't ready to try to explain.

She eventually coaxed him through the door. She asked, "Which was your first project, after you fixed the shack?" He could tell by the look in her eyes and the tone of her voice that she wasn't making fun of him. She playfully grabbed his shoulders from behind and turned him in a circle. He really couldn't remember which was his first. He had so many things he tried at first. His basic lack of knowledge of the techniques were issues he'd had to overcome. He finally reached out and grabbed a stickman type figure and said, "I think this was my first."

"How about this one?" she asked. He started to explain about it and other pieces as she held them up, including how he had painted them. She didn't realize it, but she was beaming like a little girl.

As he moved around the room, he turned on a lantern. She saw the sofa she thought was taken to the dump years ago. He was like a different man, so alive, talking about all his experiences and how he had learned to do this or that.

He turned toward her. He knew by her touches that he would have to explain the rest at another time. Could he do this? In the sanctuary that had witnessed so much of personal expression, so much emotion. He felt almost like a traitor to himself as their lips came together but, began to relax as their arms and hands covered clothing and then skin as if it were a new sensory experience. Their bodies finally joined together in a familiar way, but with a passion that was anything but familiar. There was one huge difference, she was leading. She muttered something he couldn't understand, then clearly spoke to him how sorry she was for everything she'd done. She hadn't meant to hurt him. "I promise that'll never happen again." Now she was crying.

He didn't know what to say, but finally whispered, "Does that mean, I won't have any more Tuesdays?"

14

~

Unexpected

Fed up with losing so many of his ducks to predators, he thought about what he could do to protect those he had left. The little shed they were housed in had been reinforced so tightly, it was difficult for him to get in.

A friend who trapped thought it was raccoons. Another thought it might be bobcats. He bought a trap that could handle either one. That way he would trap them, drive a distance away and release them. After a brief explanation from a trapper friend on what to use for bait, he set it up.

The next morning, he checked the trap—nothing. The following morning, still nothing even though there were obvious signs that animals had been there. The lid of the metal garbage can that held the corn was off and laid across the top of the trap. Some trapper he was.

This time he mixed corn with the peanut butter and moved the trap, so it was impossible to avoid. The next morning, he stopped as he went outside. There was a rattling noise coming from the shed. He had finally caught something. What was it?

The excitement was building as he approached the shed. He rounded the corner and quickly ducked back before he got sprayed.

This was not what was killing his ducks. This was not what was taking the lid off a metal trash can and eating the grain. Now what do you do with a skunk?

The look on his face when he walked into the house must have said it all. His wife asked him what was wrong. After he told her, he could see she was trying to stifle the laughter before she just erupted. At this point, there really wasn't much else to do but laugh with her and wonder aloud how to get the skunk out of the shed so he could feed the ducks.

Once the laughter subsided, he contacted his trapper friend. After explaining what had happened, he asked for suggestions of what to do next. He was told to approach the trap slowly and talk soothingly to the skunk, so it got used to him. Then he was to drop a large cloth over the entire trap: it wouldn't spray once it was covered. Then he could pick up the trap and dispose of it. He wasn't sure whether his friend was just playing with him or not. He decided that he was serious and left, more uncertain than when he came.

While he looked for an old shower curtain, he knew his wife was watching. She didn't say anything, but he could tell. She hadn't paid that much attention to what he was doing in a long time. What he didn't know was that she had already called their sons and most everyone they knew to describe her husband's dilemma.

Finally, he found the shower curtain. It was with some things set aside for a garage sale his wife put together three or four years ago. He started out to the shed. As he approached, he practiced how he would drop the shower curtain over the trap. In the house, all of his movements were being recorded by his wife and sent via internet before he even returned to the house. With all the appropriate misleading captions, of course.

He spread the curtain out before he rounded the corner only to find the skunk in firing position. He quickly withdrew but saw there was now a shovel he had used to block access lying across the trap. He decided to wait. He would start talking so it would get used to him. Moving so the skunk could see him, he tried not to appear threatening. It seemed to be working because the skunk would move around the trap after a while and lay down. He kept moving in closer and letting the skunk settle down until he was almost within distance. But when he brought the curtain out, that was it. The skunk turned with a purpose, as he fled.

He decided this wasn't accomplishing anything so he would mow the orchard. You don't realize how stupid your actions are sometimes until you're forced to find a way out of them. He was there and knew it wasn't worth getting sprayed by a skunk.

After he finished mowing, he came back. The skunk knew now what he was doing and wanted nothing to do with him. He put the lawn mower away and decided to try again tomorrow.

When he went into the house, his wife looked at him like an expectant child waiting for a treat. He picked up the mail and went through it.

Finally, his wife couldn't stand it anymore and blurted out, "Well?"

He looked at her as if surprised but knew full well what she was trying to get him to say. Instead, he said, "Well, what?"

"What are you and your mighty cape going to do next?" she asked, almost succeeding in containing her laughter.

Oh, she didn't have to say it that way. She was having too much fun with this. He looked at her and finally said, "I'll try again tomorrow."

"Does that mean you're going to feed it tonight?" That was all she could say before bursting out into laughter. By now the various story lines and one-liners from everyone was a story in itself. He even had to turn the volume up on the TV to hear the commentators during the football game because of all the laughter coming from the computer room.

The next morning was a cool one. He walked to the shed with the shower curtain ready. The skunk was curled up. He walked in as quiet as possible, lowered the material over the trap and removed the shovel. Only then did he realize how hard his heart was beating and his legs shaking. "Now what?" he thought. If he carried the trap to the field, how would he let it out without getting sprayed? It was starting to move around a lot, he knew he had to do something fast. He picked up the trap and started for the pond.

This was something he didn't want to do, but he could think of nothing else at the moment. As he approached the pond, he had to lift up the trap, so the cloth did not catch on the tall grass and get pulled off. Then he slipped on the wet grass going down the bank causing the trap to hit him in the chest.

Panic wasn't the appropriate word for how he felt, but it was close. He took a second to catch his breath before he reached out as far as he could to set the trap in the water. The water wasn't deep enough to submerge it. He looked around and found a stick to push the trap out further, but the trap caught on the grass and rolled over. When it did, the latch holding the door shut fell down allowing it to open and the skunk to walk out. All of a sudden, there was movement under the shower curtain headed right towards him. There could be only one thing doing that.

This time he had no trouble getting up the bank. He looked back only once before quickly reaching the house. Even though it was cold outside, he was perspiring profusely. He couldn't see the skunk but wasn't about to look for it either.

Going into the house he heard the water running in the bathroom. His wife was taking a shower. She hadn't seen any of it. A broad smile appeared on his face as he took a seat at the table. How was she going to end her story now?

15

∽

American Made

Jay loved what he did. He grew up in this store. As the last customer of the day was closing the door to leave, he knew it wouldn't be long before he may have to consider closing the door for good.

Johnson's Hardware had been in Independence for over eighty years. It wasn't always just hardware. There was once a blacksmith shop complete with grain service for the livestock. That's where the rental equipment area was now. The area that housed the Post Office originally was converted to the store's office. That was one of his first jobs when he was growing up. He would help sort the mail because so many of the hardware items were too heavy for him. His duties also included keeping the bulk area clean. Maybe that wasn't the right name for it, but that was what he called it. The nails and bolts came in big boxes and metal pail-type containers. When customers wanted nails or bolts, they had to take them out of the boxes, weigh the nails or count the bolts and put them in bags. Often, they would drop some, leaving a mess on the floor. He became an expert on the different bolt and nail sizes by picking them up and putting them in the boxes where they belonged. Often his Dad and Grandfather would tell the customers to ask Jay to show them where the bolts or nails they were looking for were.

That had all changed. Anyone could buy bolts where they bought toothpaste or wrenches when buying groceries. Often the products were inferior and sold at higher prices, but people didn't seem to care about quality or cost anymore. They called it convenience when you could go into one store and leave with whatever you wanted. It didn't matter if it was a loaf of bread or a leaf blower. Quality and specialization had become obsolete.

Yet people would stop by his store to see if he could repair these various items purchased at the box store. He quickly discovered that the cost to fix them was often more than buying new ones. The products were "throw away" items never meant to be repaired: from a trimmer to a lawn mower, some brands just couldn't be repaired. The items he sold could be repaired. Those same people who came in and complained, he would later see with new throw away products while he was on his way home. All the talk about how long they had the previous item was gone. Each time Jay would think: if they only bought it here, they wouldn't have to replace it.

This town used to have everything that was needed downtown within walking distance. Now there are a couple of restaurants and the original bank, but there isn't much left downtown aside from this store. The main branch of the bank is downtown but they're building a new branch office out by the mall. The two clothing stores were the first to leave. The pharmacy closed early last year. One of the funeral homes even closed down. That building has a day care center in it now.

There was talk for a while of one of those stores that sold things for around a dollar coming downtown where the pharmacy had been located. The mall owners somehow organized to prevent that from happening. One building had open space where a pet store used to be, but the rent the mall owner wanted was too high, so they didn't locate here at all.

People come from three area communities to shop. There is little left in their communities except to get gas and go to church. His children saw how the large stores carrying a wide variety of products could eliminate small stores, no matter how good your service was. They never mentioned getting into the business like he had, even though they each loved it, except Jane. She wanted to open a fabric store. Fortunately, she got a teaching degree. She teaches in the next town where the downtown community has nothing left. The people there are all coming over here to the mall since there aren't any businesses left in the downtown area. Just some nice old buildings waiting for someone to rescue them. With these lost businesses, local economies have lost most of their base which affects the town taxes to employment. People used to be able to walk to work, not anymore. Residents have become aware of what's happening because it is so widespread. With so many manufacturing jobs relocating outside the U.S., it has become hard for his store to purchase strictly "American Made Products" to sell.

Eventually, above his "Proudly Selling American Made Products", he tacked a smaller sign reading "When Available." People actually laughed at that; most aren't laughing at it anymore. You wonder, "How can a country responsible for so much, be left now with so little?" Industry was what helped build this country. No more.

He looked around. There were so many memories of watching his Grandfather repair leather items. So much has changed since his father took over the store. Horses were pretty much a thing of the past and now you needed parts and pieces for all the new items for repair. He remembered representatives from various companies holding informational sessions for the various stores in the region so each store owner could stay up to date on the new product lines.

At the end of each day, he would do as his Grandfather and Father had done before him. Take a walk around the store. If something was out of place, he put it where it belonged. That didn't happen very often. It was mostly just to look and take a mental inventory of items that were getting low, so he could include them with any orders. It was relaxing to know that he was the third generation to view some of the items, since the tools they replaced were now obsolete yet needed for anyone looking for a part for an older piece of equipment. How long could he continue to keep the store open; he wondered some days. Fortunately, those days were very few. But he needed to be realistic too. Jay was in his early 50s. Not a time in life to be training for a new profession.

* * *

Jay was proud to walk to work almost every morning. As he rounded the corner to Main Street, he could see the Johnson Hardware Store sign. Today it had another sign in the window that read: Retirement Sale. It had been a rough five years. He was the last business left downtown. Some who came in to look around for bargains hadn't been in the store for eight to ten years. Some bought several items they couldn't get at the big box stores or had to wait for delivery if they ordered the parts over the internet. The internet was the main reason he had made the decision he did. The internet was going to change how everyone did business. That he was sure of.

While waiting on customers, he could hear what people were saying which included: "Pretty young to be retiring." "Store hasn't changed in twenty years, maybe that's why they're closing." "You could always come in here and find what you were looking for. We're going to miss this store." "Wow, I didn't realize the tools were so inexpensive." "Can you believe all the choices they have here? Why didn't we come here before this?"

Some days he would leave the store so frustrated by what he heard. Yet other days, people were surprised they could find what they were looking for. It was like they didn't expect to find what they needed.

The store was like a virtual museum for Jay. He probably learned to walk in the store since his mother had helped there too.

There was absolutely no traffic downtown anymore. The daycare was the last to relocate, which had become a popular word. They moved to the former Baptist Church building early last year. If he wanted a sandwich, he now had to drive to one of the restaurants out by the mall. What buildings downtown that could be converted were being made into apartments, while others just stood vacant.

The former grocery store was now used to store some of the equipment for the Fire Department until their new building by the mall was finished. The small town that he knew was dying. People used to make a living wage that could support a family. Now these places were paying minimum wage with little to no insurance coverage. Before, most of the money made by a small business stayed in the area, but now it was sent to corporate headquarters, wherever that was. There was little left of the community he grew up in. A place where he had proudly raised a family and, until a few years ago, felt would be a place he would retire to. He wasn't so sure he could say that anymore since it was becoming more like living in an evolving community graveyard. All there was left were memories and that wasn't enough. Family friends were even moving out of town to downsize.

* * *

The large auction sign hung just below the Johnson Hardware Store sign. The day had come as most had been expecting. Jay had been told that people were talking around town about how several were going to control bidding so everyone would leave with bargains. The owner of another hardware store had called him earlier asking about different items. Jay called him back. The owner and several of his employees came over to look at what he had. After a brief discussion and a quick inventory, the owner was happy to take what merchandise Jay had left at a price that was fair to both of them. The only things that would be for sale would be empty shelves, some furniture, office equipment and some of those throw away tools and equipment that people had brought in for repair but never paid for. The three days set aside to prepare for the auction allowed them to remove the remaining merchandise. He was surprised nobody saw their truck being loaded, everything except the reconditioned tools. As the truck pulled away, he thought, "Well, if they want bargains, that's what they'll get."

On the day of the auction, the people were told that because of the type of items they were selling, for security reasons, they couldn't have people mulling around them and have items come up missing. That seemed to be an explanation most people understood so they took a seat in the chairs provided by the auctioneer.

When the auction started, the auctioneer explained that the shelving items were going to be sold first, then the furniture, office equipment and finally the hardware items. The shelving and furniture items sold quickly, but a lot of the office equipment was old and received no bids so Jay told the auctioneer that he would donate the office equipment that didn't sell to local churches. When it was finally announced that the hardware items were going to be sold next, several people said similar things such as "Now we get the bargains," at which time the staff working the auction brought out the repaired tools and equipment. The auctioneer said, "OK, all you bargain hunters, let's start with this reconditioned leaf blower."

To Jay's disbelief, it all sold. When the last piece of reconditioned equipment sold, the auctioneer slammed his gavel on the desk proclaiming the end of the auction. He thanked everyone for coming to a roomful of stunned faces.

"Where is all the hardware stuff?" someone asked.

The auctioneer replied, "Johnson Hardware Store was here for more than 85 years. Those that needed quality hardware items came into the store and purchased them. Mr. Johnson would like to thank every one of those customers and would like to also let you know that if you need quality hardware items, Seymour Hardware can meet your needs."

"But that's over forty miles away," a man in the front row blurted out above the chaotic clamor that followed.

"Again, thank you for coming. This auction is over," the auctioneer repeated.

Jay watched it all unfold in front of him as he sat in his office. The auctioneer spoke kind words to Jay as he waved while leaving. He and he alone knew how hard this was for Jay. His family had always taken so much pride in providing quality products and service.

Jay purposely waited in his office until everyone had left. He was glad his family had decided not to come to the auction. That would have been too hard on everyone. He knew they were planning on being here tomorrow when the sign company came to take the family sign down. He wasn't supposed to know that, but the caterer had called to make sure the building would be open.

Jay slowly walked out of the office and turned to the front door. With tears in his eyes, he drew a pocketknife from his pocket. Why did he have to close this chapter on his family's name? Slowly he began to scrape the "Proudly Selling American Made Products" sign off the door. "No reason to keep this symbol anymore."

16

∾

Decoration

Mertie was on her way to the Grand Opening of a new discount store. She was thinking about how nice it was to finally have a choice of where to shop again. Oops, there are flashing lights, she better pullover to let them by. She didn't know how long he had been behind her. Maybe there was an accident across town.

The patrol car didn't pass her but pulled up behind her. The young officer got out and asked, "Can I see your license and registration?"

"Well, it's right in my glove compartment over there," she said, as if he should know where people keep those things.

"Yes ma'am," he said before continuing, "but can I see them?"

"What for, young man? Don't you believe me? Why do you have those flashing lights on? Is somebody in trouble?"

"No," was all he was able to reply before she cut him off by saying, "Then why don't you just go and shut them off. People are going to think there is something wrong!"

"I turned them on because you were going too fast in a school zone, Myrtle," he said.

She read his name tag, Robinson. "Are you Stella's son?" she asked.

"Grandson," he said.

"I bet she is proud of you. I just talked to her last night. She asked me if I wanted to go with her to the new store, but she wasn't going until this afternoon. Oh, I'm so excited. Have you been yet?"

"No," he replied.

"Well, it was sure good to meet you again, but I've got to get going," she said as she pulled away. To her amazement, that young man followed her. "Fortunately, he had turned off those lights," she thought. Maybe there was a traffic problem at the new store.

She was able to find a parking spot. There were no problems she could see, yet he pulled up next to her. She got out and walked over to his car where he was writing something and asked, "Are you going in too? If you are, I'll wait for you. If you're not going to be too long."

"No," he said. "I just followed to make sure you got here safely. Have a nice day, Myrtle," then he pulled away.

"That's Mertie, young man," she tried to correct him, but she wasn't sure he heard her. She turned and started for the store. She was almost to the front door when she realized she didn't have her purse. Begrudgingly, she returned to her car and got her purse. Now she was ready.

When she got inside, she walked over and got a cart. She wasn't sure why since she was just going to buy her favorite cereal. So why was she in the toy aisle now? Just looking around, she reminded herself.

Before she knew it, she had the train set her grandson wanted for Christmas and things for two of the three grand-daughters. She was surprised this store had what she was looking for and for less than that other discount store or even the internet. She wasn't so sure on that last part, but that was what everyone was talking about. She wasn't so good on the computer. They wouldn't get much of her business since she had to rely on her grandkids to even check her mail. Why did they call it mail if they made it so hard to get to?

She finally made it to the cereal aisle where she was able to buy three boxes of cereal for the normal price of two. Wow, she liked this store.

As she made it through the checkout, she was already planning for her next trip. When she came out into the parking lot, she was surprised by how full it was. She headed to where she had parked, only, where had she parked? She was relieved she had kept the cart because she never would have been able to carry all her purchases. Besides that, she had something to lean on.

She wandered around embarrassed about her predicament. She remembered how it had always bothered her when her husband would put one of those "Antenna Ornaments" on their car. Especially that last one that was a lime green colored ball. It looked like a miniature tennis ball and he didn't even play tennis.

Her new car didn't even have an antenna. If it did, maybe she could break down and find one that was more tasteful. "How can you lose a car in a parking lot?" She hated to even think about it, but maybe her daughter was right when she asked her not to go shopping alone.

She lived alone, who did she think was going to go with her? Maybe it would have been better to have waited and shopped with Stella. Then she would've had company looking for her car.

A voice spoke out from behind her which caught her totally off guard. "Can I help you?" She turned and saw a total stranger.

"Yes," she explained. "I can't find my car."

He smiled and said, "I've done that before myself. I used to have something on my antenna, but my new car doesn't have one, so I try and park by a light pole now. I figure there are only so many of them, I won't have to look in too many places." They both laughed before he continued, "So many of these big stores now have one area where you enter and another where you exit. Often, they are not even close to where you parked to go into the store leaving you totally disoriented. What color is your car?"

"Well, it's a silver-colored sedan," she said.

"That pretty much describes about a third of the vehicles here in the parking lot," and they laughed again.

"It does, doesn't it," she replied.

"Wait," he said. "Do you have your car keys?" he asked.

"Of course, how do you think I got here? Well, it doesn't really take a key," she said. "It's just one of those you have to have with you to let you start it. My husband would turn over in his grave if he knew they made something that didn't require a key."

"I understand," he said before continuing, "but do you have

it with you? The reason I'm asking is they usually have a door lock and unlock button."

"Oh, I never thought of that," she said and looked for it in her purse. When she found it, she pressed the button to lock the doors. They both heard a beep on the other side of a minivan that wasn't there when she came. They walked around it.

"Is this your car?" he asked.

"Yes. That's it. That sure beats that ugly lime colored ball we used to have on our car when my husband was alive," Mertie said and they both laughed.

He started to walk toward the store, stopped and said, "My wife never liked our car decoration either. She always tried to find one that nobody else had, which at times was interesting. Now that I know using the key works, I won't be one of the only one's parking way back by those light poles anymore. Thank you. Have a good day."

17

～

Faded Red Wagon

They were headed for Watertown when they came upon an Amish farmer going up a hill. They slowed down since it wasn't safe to pass. The wagon behind the Amish horses was just a simple wooden wagon, but similar to one his family used while he was growing up. That one was a faded red color, probably painted with milk paint. This one was not painted but loaded with firewood.

He remembered putting oats into the spreader with a small toy shovel while his mother drove the tractor. He was barely tall enough to hold onto the top of the spreader and the end gate of the wagon to keep his balance. He felt so important. This allowed his father to drive the other tractor with the roller to force the seed into the soil. This gave the seed a better chance of surviving the flock of birds following behind them.

They used the red wagon to pick up rocks, which there were always plenty of, then carry seed corn and soybeans to the planter. The wagon also carried hay or newborn calves to the barn if they were born in the pasture.

Here he was over fifty years later, following a piece of equipment that made the past feel like it happened yesterday, even if it had metal wheels. The team of horses used here was also different than the John Deere A his family used. It was also more than 1,200 miles from where he grew up in Iowa.

He remembered how some neighbors bought big shiny steel wagons to carry the different types of seed to the planters. They also used them to harvest. Families that didn't buy these big wagons had to pay extra for bagged seed.

Soon the wooden wagons started to disappear as if people were ashamed to use them. After a while, even ours was relegated to just hauling in the wood. A used pickup replaced it to perform its other duties.

The wagon that was such a part of everything our family did was left by the wood pile. An embarrassing relic left to rot away. Forgotten until...

"Hon," he heard his wife say again.

"Wha... What?" he said.

"Are you alright or just waiting for the next hill?"

18

Red Velvet Chair

Stoic like its former owner. Comfortable like an old pair of jeans. The red velvet chair sat in the corner of the library amongst the metal and fiberglass furniture of its new owners, Ben and Toni Mason. They needed to decide on what to do with it and they both knew it. Finally, Ben said, "Toni, we have to talk. Do we keep it or give it away? It just doesn't fit in the library."

Toni looked up at him, "I thought you would eventually give in if we waited long enough." She had just fed their newborn son, Eric, who was almost asleep. The chair was a prized possession of hers. When she and her brother were growing up, her grandfather read to them in that chair. "We both agree that it doesn't fit with our things in the library like it did at Gramps. Each worn spot has a history to it whether it was made from Grandpa reading to us or my brother and I sitting there by ourselves. With hours of imaginary adventure, the chair requires its own special place. One where we can pass that love of reading on to Eric. Ben, that's all I'm asking. That's why I suggested our bedroom."

Ben would have nothing to do with the chair being placed in the bedroom. He couldn't explain it even to himself, but he tried. "I just don't want the chair in our bedroom because..." he paused. "Because there are times that I feel I'm being watched when working on my lesson plan. I know that sounds stupid, but I certainly don't want to have that feeling in our bedroom." He was embarrassed to admit it. He finally stammered,

"How about in our entryway? It has a lot of room if we find another place for that small table."

"That's an idea. Let's put Eric to bed and then look at it."

Ben cherished being a father and couldn't wait until Eric was older. Eric's life was mainly food and excreting. Changing diapers was one thing, but he couldn't wait to teach Eric how to throw a ball or ride a bike. Ben never knew his father. He had to watch other fathers teaching their kids how to throw a ball or ride a bike without appearing to intrude. He still remembers how left out he felt. That wasn't going to happen to any of his kids.

Together they walked into the entryway and over to the front door, looking back into the small room. "Can you move the table?" Toni asked.

Ben set the table around the corner in the kitchen. "There is a lot of room," Toni said out loud, but it was meant only for herself since Ben had made this suggestion several months ago. "Ok, let's try it," she proclaimed.

Ben was back so fast with the chair that she was about to ask him if he would move the—It fit. She smiled before asking, "But where can we put Eric's books?"

Ben looked at her and said, "I think there is enough room to put a bookshelf along here," as he pointed to an area along the wall. "I think I can build one similar to the one in our bedroom, but smaller so he can reach the books."

"That would be great," she said as she sat down to take it all in. She would have to figure out what she could do to make it special. She thought about the gumball machine Grandpa found. For a penny, you could get a gumball. Once you had the gumball, the penny would fall out on the floor. It became as much fun watching to see how far the penny would roll as it was getting the gumball. That was until Gramps found a wad of gum stuck to the bottom of the velvet chair. Then the treats became hard candy. She would look for something just as unique.

* * *

It took Ben about a week to find the time to build and finish Eric's bookshelf. He was also able to find a floor lamp that didn't look modern yet didn't look cheap, even though it was.

Toni added a little stand that had various animals that Eric loved. She stood back with her arms around Ben who was holding Eric and said, "Grandpa would be proud."

It did look nice. As the months went by, Ben would find them sitting in the chair whether she was nursing Eric or reading to him. It was hard to imagine how many books had been read to him. Ben knew it was probably more than had been read to him in his entire childhood.

One night, Toni came into the library where Ben was working on a lesson plan and said. "Ben, I don't know how to explain it, but when we are sitting there, it is almost like the old velvet chair is alive. I feel so warm and protected. Can that be for real or do you think it is just because that was the way I felt with Grandpa?"

"I don't know, but if I were to guess," he started, "I would say it could be a learned experience. When Eric is fussing and you take him out there and sit down, it isn't very long, and he quiets right down whether you're reading to him or not. Could it be that you're more relaxed and he can sense that? I don't know but I have noticed this...." he paused as if trying to think of something else to say but found himself just trying to make sense of what he just said. "I don't know. I know I had some feelings in the library I told you about, but I can't explain why I felt them. I didn't have the history with the chair you've had."

They both smiled. "Are you ready to put Eric to bed?" Toni asked.

"Yes, I'm glad you're comfortable with this, Hon, as he laid down his papers. It's almost like I'm going through a childhood while learning to be a father. I don't remember any of these experiences from my youth. Besides, I'm a little jealous of the close bond that you and Eric have developed. I know this is just temporary but it's truly special."

"Yes, it is," Toni said. "To think of how anxious, I was of being a mother at first. It couldn't be more natural." Ben saw her tears starting to form and drew her close. Quietly, he guided them down the hallway to Eric's room.

She watched as he carefully took their son in his arms. The importance of the word "their" suddenly became magnified. "Their son" did respond differently to Ben's touch than to hers. She was surprised that even at this young age, Eric already knew the difference between them. She knew that she was going to have to modify the feeding routine because she would soon have to return to work. That meant she was going to have to leave him. She wasn't ready for that.

Ben handed Eric back to her, interrupting her thoughts. He hoped she hadn't noticed his tears. Why was he such a lump when it came to things like this? He never used to be.

She smiled, kissed him and said, "Welcome back, Benny," knowing full well he didn't like to be called that.

Instead of finding Ben in the library, he was standing in the entry looking at the cat and birdie book she had read to Eric. "You know you can sit down," she said, but he remained standing. "My body doesn't fit in that chair," he said.

"Real funny," she said. She paused as he faked a hurt look. "Have you ever read anything that Grandpa wrote?" she asked.

"No, I know that he wrote, but I've never read any of his writings."

"I'd like to read you one of his poems that still makes me feel like a little girl." She walked over to the bookcase, picked up a book saying, "We had a swing set in our yard. I just loved to swing so he wrote this for me. It is called, "Up, Up, In The Air." She stopped and took a breath before continuing:

> She sat in the swing as it went
> back and forth on a cool Fall day.
> Her hair fell onto her face hiding it,
> then away as if it was trying to flee.
> She rocked her head back and said,
> "Up, up, in the air."
> She stopped as if to listen
> before she started to sing,

Up, up, in the air.
She adjusted the soft tone
with that of the birds as if
they were serenading each other.

Ben looked at the youthful smile on her face and then the tears started. Ben took her in his arms, engulfing her much like he had done earlier with Eric. Even though the night was young, she escorted him towards their bedroom. He shuffled clumsily past the living room where the sounds from the TV indicated the Giants' game was on. He never even flinched.

She led. She was soft and slow yet definitely in charge, letting Ben know exactly what she wanted. They loved each other as if they wanted to hold on to each sensation their bodies created before experiencing the next.

When they finally lay in silence, they both realized their relationship was changing. Ben's smile was too obvious to miss as he thought of how Toni had finally taken charge. He felt so close to her.

While Toni, for the first time since her pregnancy, felt Ben had finally loved her with passion. Even though her body didn't look the same, she was the same person and needed him more than before. The thought that he looked at her differently now was gone. He had loved her totally.

* * *

Even though Ben had always helped with the household chores, he now took pride in doing the different duties. He had changed. He wasn't sure how, but he could feel it. "So, this is what it was like to be a part of a family," he thought.

Eric was crawling now and making sounds. Of course, they both interpreted Eric's various sounds that began with D or M as "Daddy" or "Mommy." Toni had returned to work. Even though they were glad their babysitter was Toni's mother, Grace, they both felt they were missing the baby's "firsts."

One day Grace had to leave early for a doctor's appointment. Toni couldn't get off because she didn't have any more vacation time, but Ben did. Eric was now close to walking. When Toni arrived home, Ben was in the red chair with Eric on his lap reading him a story. She had never seen Ben in that chair. Not that she hadn't tried to get him to sit in it, but it was her place. Or was it? "Mommy," Eric said, "Daddy ook."

Ben saw the look on her face. He was surprised by her expression, but when Eric spoke, her expression lightened. "Would you like to finish reading this?" Ben asked.

"How about if I join you two in the chair? I'd love to finish reading, but you aren't getting away just because I'm here." Quickly, she sat on Ben's knee and then noticed there were only three pages left. She turned to Eric, kissed him on the forehead before she dramatically turned to the book and read,

"The monkey looked at his friends

They were all eating a banana."

"Nanna. Nanna Mommy," Eric said.

"Do you think we should all share a banana like the monkeys?" she asked. "Yes," Eric cried happily. "Let's go see if we can find one," Toni said as she picked Eric up and headed to the kitchen.

Ben sat looking at the worn spots on the velvet arms of the chair. He must have been about the same size as Toni's grandfather since the chair's arms seemed to welcome his. With the quality of the velvet, it must have taken hours and hours of special moments to cause these worn areas. Where his head rested, the indenture in the padding fit his neck and head perfectly. He didn't have to look at the worn area to know, he could feel it. He felt like he belonged in it. He hated to admit it, but the chair did have a calming effect. Although he wasn't prepared to announce, "It's almost as if it is alive."

Suddenly he looked up. To his embarrassment, his eyes met Toni and Eric standing in the doorway looking at him. Just then he realized his private moment was anything but that.

"Nanna Daddy?"

19

❧

Gift

A blue pickup pulled into the driveway. A young man got out and asked, "Are you Tom?"

"Yes, I am. How can I help you?" he said.

"My name is Ray Clark. We live just around the corner. Our family has raised two geese, but we don't have a pond for them. Since you have a pond, would we be willing to adopt them?"

"How much do you want for them?" Tom asked.

"Nothing," Ray said. We have chickens and other small animals, but we hadn't planned on the geese outgrowing their kiddie swimming pool as fast as they have. They really need a pond to swim in. If it is alright, we will bring them right over."

"We'll be home all day," Tom said.

When Ray came back, his daughter was with him. He grabbed the pet carrier and walked toward the pond with his daughter beside him. He stopped, set the carrier down and opened the cage door. The geese cautiously walked out, looked around, but then came over to the girl, who bent over and pet the biggest one. He stood there as if expecting her to rub his other side. "They should be just fine with your ducks," Ray said.

"They should be," Tom said as he walked the rest of the way to the pond. As the geese walked towards him and the water, the young father and daughter took the opportunity to get into the vehicle and drove off. As Tom moved out on some rocks that were at the edge of the pond, the geese stayed with him on the shoreline. They were looking at him and wondering what in the world he was doing. What should they be doing? That was when he realized, they didn't know what the water was. He stood there laughing as the red winged blackbirds flew by overhead, unhappy about their space being violated.

He walked back to the shed with the geese following him. Picked up the canoe and a paddle and carried it down to the pond. After setting the canoe in the water, he climbed in. The geese started trying to get into the canoe with him, so he pushed off a few feet from shore.

This caused such a clamor of honking from the geese that one of them was knocked into the water. It tried to get back on shore but then, the other one fell in. They both looked at each other, then at him. They then tried to pull a walking on water act as fast as they could. After reaching the canoe, they tried to get in the canoe with him but couldn't. Giving up, they hooked their necks over the edge of the canoe as if that was going to save them. He started to paddle slowly out onto the pond. They never left the side of the canoe but did start to swim. This pattern went on for over a week before they finally swam on their own.

Tom learned quickly, that unless he locked them up for the night, they were going where he went. That is why he stopped using the front door. The geese started coming on the porch and he couldn't get them off. If the door was open, the cat would taunt them by walking by the door. As they got used to that, it would then come and lay by the door stretched out. When they got bored, they would spread their wings acting like they were about to attack, which usually sent the cat running. They finally reached a truce and would just stare at each other.

Unfortunately, by using the back door, they were introduced to the garden. The peas were the first to be discovered and were now pretty much unrecognizable. The tomato plants were next. The young fruit that was forming pretty much disappeared shortly after the blossom stage. Next to be discovered were the red raspberries. Tom didn't have to worry about bending over to pick the ones near the ground now because there weren't any.

Recently, when he was painting the trim on the house, he sat down in the shade to cool off. They came over just talking away in goose language as if he understood everything that was being said. Pretty soon, they laid down in the grass right beside him. "Just when you think about trying to find them a new home, they do something like this," he thought. When he told his wife about the red raspberries, he thought that would be the last straw, especially after one of them nipped her while she was bringing in groceries.

"Should we find them a new home?" he asked.

"Why?" she said. "Isn't that why they have Farmers' Markets?"

20

Picture of Life

The cottonwood leaves rustled in the stifling heat in the dog days of August. The majestic oaks still dominate the ridge and act as guardians of what lies in between them and the meandering creek. He had been coming here occasionally for as long as he could remember with his Grandpa and his dad. He would play with his toy truck in the dirt piles they made just for him.

Occasionally, his Grandpa found a small stone that was shaped like an egg. He would give these little rocks to him but would call them dinosaur eggs. They fit perfectly in the palm of the boy's hand. When he started school, he took several of his favorite ones with him. There was a little girl who lived on a farm and started bringing some in too. That was until some of the kids started to make fun of them for not knowing they were just rocks.

That didn't stop either of them from collecting them. Soon there were several classmates collecting them and showing each other new ones on the playground. Each had special places they would put them. He put his in a pile near his mother's flower garden so his Grandpa could see them every time he visited. It's a habit he continues today at his home, even though Grandpa has been deceased now for several years. When he sees that pile, it automatically brings back memories as varied as the stones. It's a tradition he has passed on to his own son, but they are no longer called dinosaur eggs. They are each a stone with a special message all their own for the person who has them. He wasn't sure if his son understood at first until he overhead his son telling his older sister about several of them. What an imagination, he thought and smiled.

His father had always liked being in the background. In fact, when taking a picture was even mentioned, he would usually flee the eye of the camera saying, "If I can recognize myself when I look into the mirror, that's all I need." There were literally years without a photographic record of his dad during that time period for the family album.

When he got ill, they didn't expect it since he had always been so strong. Now he was removing a wooden frame from the back of the truck. Not for just anyone, but for his father. When he opened it, he remembered how puzzled he was the first time he saw it. He had asked, "What is that for Grandpa?"

His Grandpa had looked at him, thought for a second and said, "It's so we can create a deep picture." "Why do you want to create a deep picture, Grandpa?" he asked. "You'll see when we make it. Now go play," Grandpa said as he went for more tools.

He didn't understand what his grandfather meant until he was much older and became a part of the team. Like painters who choose their tools according to the work, the grave diggers did too. They had no concerns over colors though. For them, it was an array of shovels, picks and even an axe for the odd prairie tree roots.

Now he had taken over the grave digging for the community cemetery. Today was different. He was alone for a reason. This was no ordinary task. This was personal. It was for the man who had given him life. The man who had taught him most of what he knew. He would have done most anything for him, even though he had faults that sometimes hurt those he loved the most. This was for his Father. Now it was his honor to produce a picture that his Dad would have been proud of.

When done, a copy of the obituary would be placed directly under where the casket would rest. If they found any rocks, they would place them evenly along the head and toe of the grave. A favorite beverage would be placed in the left corner if a man or in the right corner if a woman. He remembered asking Grandpa why? He told him, "That's because the women are usually right. Even if you go to a public restroom, the women's is usually on the right."

As his dad grew older, he began to personalize the graves even more. If a person was a teacher, he would add things in the walls and in the bottom of the grave that they would have used during their lifetime. He had trouble with people that he didn't know since he had no idea what their lives were like. Those were the modest pictures. He loved it when the individual had been a farmer. There were so many different things he could use to develop the background of the picture.

Now physically and mentally exhausted, he walked slowly back to the truck. He didn't want to use a tractor for this one, even though he could have. The passenger seat was full since his father was a farmer, a mechanic and an artist. By the time he was done, his creation would be covered by a carpet for the funeral. No one would see it. He thought of taking a picture. This one was too personal. He didn't want to second guess the tribute he'd created of his Father's picture of life.

21

∽

Last One Standing

"John, have you ever thought of remarrying?"

"No. I haven't Ed."

"Why not?" Ed asked.

"Just never thought I'd be the last one standing. There have been times I've thought about finding a friend though," John replied.

"I know what you mean. Millie had so many relatives that lived into their nineties, I never once thought I'd be the one that would be left behind."

"You know, Ed, my worry was whether I would get to know the grandkids. With the war and all, we had kids later in life. Then our kids waited to have children. When most people were thinking of great grandchildren, we were welcoming grandchildren."

"At least you get to babysit yours. My grandchildren live in other states. They're in their teens now and about ready to leave home to be on their own. When I see them, they're so busy with their other things that I get very little 'us' time. I miss that," Ed said, looking off toward the kids on the swings.

"Is that why you like to meet here in the park?" John asked.

"I guess that is part of it," Ed said, thinking before he continued. "Initially I came here to get to know you. I'd been watching you and your granddaughter walk over here. Then I'd see you sitting on this bench all alone while she played with the other kids. It was like you were a lamppost until she was ready to go home. It was hard for me to get up the nerve at first, but I knew I had to get out of that house and away from all those memories. They were becoming my life. Not only have you become a friend, but I've gotten to know your granddaughter a bit. By the way, I also enjoy the ice cream rewards afterwards."

"There is a little bit of a child in all of us no matter how old we are, isn't there? I'm glad you got up the nerve to pester me," John said jokingly before adding. "I am enjoying being a grandpa at the moment. When school starts, then I'll have more time to think and wonder what's next."

"You're in good health. You should look for one of those ladies who would like a friend," Ed said.

"If you consider being able to cook, walk and breathe being in good health, then I guess I am. What I find hard to accept though is how I can do something today with no problems. Six months later, I have to rest before completing the same task. Have you ever had that happen to you?"

"Yes, I have to admit I have. My first main mission was to become competent with the housework. Hell, I had to ask the next-door neighbor to show me how to operate the vacuum cleaner," Ed said laughing before continuing. "I got sick of canned soups and deli foods. Then one afternoon, I was in the grocery store when it hit me. I used to grill. Why wasn't I doing that now? That night, I brushed the snow off the grill. I had one of the best tasting steaks I'd had in a long time. Now I cook, clean and all the other things without thinking about it, so my needs have changed. Now I would just like to have someone to talk to, but not talk too much though," and they both laughed.

"When you find yourself answering your own question, you've got to laugh at yourself. At least, I do," John noted. "I do those word games to pass the time when there is nothing on TV or I don't feel like reading. It is really too soon to think about anything else. There are a couple of ladies from church who lost their husbands that have always been easy to talk to. I am not interested in remarrying again though."

"I thought about getting together with someone from work who was younger. We were always on the same page. Shortly after that, I was at a restaurant when this couple came in. She was steadying him as he walked with a cane. She was beautiful, probably close to twenty years younger than he was. They got their food about the same time as I did. When I finished, I noticed her cutting up his fish, just a little at a time. Neither of them had eaten much as she was assisting him. She was so considerate not eating any faster than he did. Maybe it was because she didn't want him to feel bad about how slow he was. In a way it was beautiful. In another, it was sad," Ed said shaking his head looking off as if the couple were right there.

"By what you have said, there is little doubt that she loved him. Yet I think I know what you mean by feeling it was unfair since she had so much more to give. How long can a young woman keep an old man young? I wasn't there, but it appears to have worked for them," John said looking over at the playground.

"I didn't look at it that way, but I can't stop thinking about how unfair it would be for the younger person. Well, it looks like she's getting ready," Ed said as he started to stand up.

John stood up with him and said, "I thought about going into one of those retirement community-type places but then I wouldn't be as close as I am to where my granddaughter lives. Maybe when she gets older...."

He stretched and waited for his granddaughter and friend to get close before asking, "Who's ready for ice cream?"

22

⌇

Spoon

With the small branches trimmed and hauled away, he cut the limbs into pieces suitable for firewood and loaded them in the trailer. He turned his attention to the crooked trunk which had failed the old maple tree in the windstorm.

As he worked his way down the log, he was careful to cut the pieces with crooks shorter to make them easier to split. He didn't own a log splitter, not yet anyway. Friends made fun of him for still splitting his firewood by axe. At first, he would feel stiff and sore but, he always felt stronger and able to split more wood faster than with a splitter. All without having to pay for a gym membership, which many of his friends did.

The rest of the log looked like it was lying flat on the ground, so he started to cut straight through. He went to pull the chainsaw out to start another cut when the saw pinched sending the saw outward. The handle struck the muscle on the inside of his knee.

He shut the chainsaw off, turned and sat on the partially cut log. Tears were streaming down his face as he put his hands around his knee. He couldn't think of anything else to do. After a while, he was able to stand up as the pain gradually dissipated. The scent brought in by the wind warned him it would soon be raining or snowing. He bent over cautiously, rolled the log over and picked up the chainsaw. Before making the final small cuts, he made sure he was not standing directly behind the saw. He knew better but had just gotten too complacent with a dangerous tool.

He couldn't remember ever taking so many precautions to make the final cuts. He was aware of where his legs were in relation to the saw. His wagon loaded, he headed home on the tractor with the once proud tree and gave thanks to the forest. It was a tradition his father had taught him.

When he got home, he parked the tractor and trailer in the shed. He didn't even bother to put the chainsaw or anything else away. His knee was really tightening up now, but he didn't dare let his wife notice. She wasn't too keen about still burning firewood, let alone him harvesting it.

She was busy, but somehow heard him open the freezer when he went to get some ice for his knee. "Don't eat that last ice cream bar. There are cookies on the counter," she said. So, of course, that meant the cookies were his, but the ice cream was hers. She'd be out soon to see what he was up to.

He quickly put the ice in a sandwich bag, went into the living room and sat down. He grabbed a lap throw to conceal the ice pack and turned on the TV, scanning between a couple of college basketball games. When she heard the games on, she went to the freezer for her ice cream, but didn't come in.

The ice felt good, but he knew he couldn't leave it on there. After about twenty minutes, he took it off, only to put it back on about a half hour later. Sometime during the evening, he had fallen asleep. He woke up to the news with his wife asking, "Who won the game?"

"Which game?" he asked knowing full well by the smirk already forming on her face that she wasn't going to buy that. She was headed for bed.

He waited until she was in bed before trying to get up. When he did, it took a lot of effort. He didn't even try to bend it. He could put weight on it but knew this wasn't going to be a silent friend. He took a pill for pain. He then let the water run a bit and filled the bag with cold water to put on his knee.

Finally, he was ready for bed. He shut the light off before he went into the bedroom. As he fumbled in the dark, he carefully got in bed.

"Are you alright?" she asked.

Dang, she doesn't miss anything he thought, before saying, "Just have a headache."

"You overexerted yourself, didn't you? You didn't even unload the trailer," she noted.

"Possibly," was all he could say which turned out to be just enough as she rolled over and was soon asleep. As he lay there, he wondered how anyone could snore peacefully like she did? Maybe her snoring would help put him to sleep. It didn't.

After an hour or so, he got up since he wasn't even close to being asleep. Fortunately, he didn't wake her. He remembered seeing ice cream in the big freezer, so he dished out a small portion, dribbled some maple syrup on it without turning on a light. He then went out to the screened-in deck to sit on the metal framed swing. The cool air felt good on his knee.

The sounds of nature were in full chorus around the pond.

Occasionally, a bull frog would try to sound as imposing as possible. Some coyotes started sporadic howling in the woods behind the orchard. The controlled howling soon turned into a feverish, uncontrolled combination of howling and cries. Then there was total silence. Even the area around the pond grew silent. Was it a tribute to whatever it was that just lost its life? He didn't know. The tribute didn't last long, but it was definitely noticeable.

After finishing his ice cream, he took in the celestial display. He was just about to reposition his leg when he noticed movement. As the movement came closer, he could see there were two people. When they got almost to his garden, he saw their hands full of tools.

All he had was a spoon and bowl in his hand, so he took the spoon and tapped the metal frame once. They both froze. Finally, he asked, "Do one of you have a cell phone?"

The one in front slowly said, "I do."

"Call 911," he heard himself saying.

"OK. Can I set this compressor down? My phone is in my left pocket."

"Yes, but set it right in front of you," he said. He watched the man set the compressor down and heard the person ask, "What should I say?"

"Identify yourself, then your friend. Tell them you are standing in the backyard at 913 Low Bridge Road with stolen tools," he said this as his mind was rushing. He watched as the phone lit up exposing the owner's face.

He heard the guy on the phone identify himself as Randy and his friend as Phil. He heard Randy repeat everything he said to the word. He then heard Randy ask, "What else should I say?"

He said nothing and didn't move even though his leg was throbbing. Fear was now very audible in Randy's voice so he raised the phone back up to his face and asked the dispatcher, "Can you stay on the phone with me until the police officers arrive?" There was a short pause before Randy continued, "We don't know, but we both heard a click. Is that alright with you mister?"

He didn't reply, but Randy again spoke into the phone. "Yes, I am still here, but this guy is like a ghost. Please hurry," Randy said. Soon the sound of sirens became audible.

As the lights from the officer's cruiser lit up his backyard, he realized he still had the spoon in his left hand. He lowered it out of sight as his wife opened the door and asked, "What's going on?"

23

Tina

She sat stone faced, which meant she was about to cry or erupt in anger. He wasn't sure which. "You want to go for a ride, Hon?" he asked.

Surprised, she looked up and then out the window before saying, "Yes, I need to get out of here, but only if we don't stop anywhere." She was in no mood for that.

He looked at her as she walked to the door and said, "You may need a coat, there was a frost on the windshield this morning. As for stopping anywhere, I just have to get a bag of dog food but that can wait until you're ready." She just nodded while putting on her coat and walked to the truck.

As they pulled out of the driveway, she thought about what they were going to do now. She couldn't think rationally about the future. "Nick, how about driving over to the park? We can get out and walk. If we're lucky, we'll see one of the freighters on the river. How does that sound?" she asked.

"That sounds fine. It'll be cold, but feel good," he replied.

There was one car in the parking area. From the car, they

could see people walking a dog on a leash. Nick and Rose decided to take the path along the river. The seagulls that were lounging along the bank didn't even bother to move as they walked within a few feet of them. They had walked this way several years ago when they realized their daughter, Tina, was thinking of becoming a teacher. They had talked then about how they were going to afford it? She would be the first from either of their families to go to college. They asked several people they worked with about investing for college and finally put money in a special savings plan with Rose's employer. They were so proud of themselves. Tina even got involved putting most of her babysitting money into the account before she got a job on the weekends. This gave her a sense of ownership in the educational savings plan, too.

That was before she met Todd. He worked at the same store she did but was going to a different school. He wanted to go to college to become an engineer. They really liked Todd and often talked to Nick and Rose about their plans. Rose had even taken Tina to the Doctor's office to ensure those dreams would become a reality. Until yesterday when Tina told her that she may have missed her period.

The personal revelation is what caused Rose to erupt and make it very public. The frustration of thinking that years of saving and preparing had all been for naught didn't help. Rose and Tina both said things they weren't proud of. She needed to think before she saw her daughter again.

Tina had worked hard in school. Her grades showed it. They had to almost force her to spend any of her money she earned to buy various things she needed. Rose hoped it wasn't going to be used now to buy a house. Rose wondered what she could have done.

Nick interrupted her thoughts when he said, "That's a big freighter. Can you see a flag?"

"No," she said. "When it clears the island tree line, we'll be able to see the name of the ship."

They both stood waiting for the ship to turn. She was relaxing, he could tell by the lines in her face and the tone of her voice. He was glad she had agreed to get away. She had really said some harsh words, but he knew they were more out of frustration than anger.

The Norwegian Fjord finally came into view. Neither of them said anything as they watched it, until it passed by the island and out of sight. They started toward the boat ramp, but at a much slower pace than before.

Nick was glad Rose had said "yes." Tina had her car. If Tina got back before he did, he wasn't sure what would happen. Especially after hearing what each of them had said the night before. He could tell by Rose's posture and the lighter sound of her shoes on the pavement that she was unwinding. Soon she would want to talk about it. Until then, he knew to wait.

It was a good thing that all of this happened on a Friday night. This gave them the weekend to work through this. He didn't want anything more said that would leave everyone sorry.

"She really hurt me," Rose finally blurted out.

"I know," was all that Nick could say.

"She came to us all alone; he didn't come with her." Rose stopped and kicked a small stone out of the path. "You were with me when we told my parents."

"Yes, I wasn't sure whether your father was going to run me off, hit me or just shoot me," Nick replied.

Rose laughed and said, "That's right, I had the same feeling, but I was so worried about Mom's reaction. Do you remember? She made both of us promise to finish high school, no matter what the other kids said."

"Then Mom asked when the baby was due. I went to the calendar and circled July. Dad melted in the chair by the table. His look of strength was replaced with a look that made him appear so frail."

"Then Mom's next statement seemed so bizarre, yet turned out to be so true when she made it clear I was going to be feeding that baby and it wasn't coming from a bottle... I remember being shocked that she would even say such a thing in mixed company. She wanted the baby to know who its mother was. She wanted me to get to know my baby. At first, I remember thinking she was just trying to punish me. Then I learned to appreciate what she meant by bonding. Mom was the babysitter during the day, but when I came home for lunch or after school, there was no doubt who Tina's mother was."

Nick nodded, "I just remember how Tina responded when she was around you. Even though at that time, I didn't have a clue what was going on. She was just so different around you than she was with me. I don't know who was prouder. Your mother or me the first time I changed her diaper." He stopped, took Rose's hand and said, "Your mother was a good teacher. Can we be the same for Tina?"

"I don't know," Rose said. "I just didn't think I'd be a grandmother at age 34. I was preparing for graduation, then

college, just like her. I just wish Todd would have been wit.
when she told me, like you were."

"Maybe he doesn't know."

"Could that be?" Rose asked.

"I know Tina hurt you when she said that she is going to
be older than you were when she was born. That hit me hard
too, thinking our daughter even knew but, then again, why
wouldn't she?" Nick said.

The cell phone rang. Rose said, "It's Tina, she must be
through with her test at the doctor's office. I don't want to take
this call and break this wonderful moment but..."

"Hello, Tina, can we talk when we get home?" and she hung
up.

Nick looked at her stunned as she quickly started to dial the
phone. "What's wrong?" he asked only to hear his wife's excited voice ask, "Tina, did you say the nurse said the test was
negative?"

24

⌇

Scotty

The air was stifling. The bugs will be bad tonight, Scotty thought, as he rounded the corner of the parking lot. With it being a weeknight and summer break, it will be a short night.

He turned towards the river to check out a swimming hole. It was late enough that the sunbathers would be gone, but early enough that the bottles and cans would still be visible.

He stopped by the big weeping willow to listen. He didn't hear anyone, so he looked around the tree. There was no one in sight so he walked to the riverbank taking a plastic bag from his rear pocket. As he started to pick up the empty water and soda bottles, he was surprised there were no empty beer bottles. This was unusual.

When the students return, it's not unusual to fill two garbage bags full Saturday and Sunday mornings after the partiers had left. Often, the kids would have most of the garbage bags filled and ready for Scotty to pick up. Officer Bishop would give him a ride to the Recycling Center. The Police Department appreciated everything he did in keeping the community and university grounds picked up.

As he topped the ridge by the river, it was Officer Murphy waiting to give him a ride. "Hi, Scotty. It's going to be a hot one tonight."

"It sure is, Mr. Murphy. The bugs'll be bad later."

"Would you like to go down by the 4th Street Bridge? There was quite a party there last night," Officer Murphy asked.

"There was? Sure. I sure appreciate that Mr. Murphy."

"Whoops. Sorry, Scotty. I have to let you out here. That car drove through that stop sign," as he stopped to let Scotty out, he turned his lights on.

"Thank you, Mr. Murphy," Scotty said, but he probably didn't hear as he sped off. He was less than two blocks from the bridge.

As he walked down to the water, he noticed what Mr. Murphy was talking about. Soon his bag was full. He brought it up to the side of the bridge before pulling out another bag from his pocket.

The articles of clothing that were there he would give to Bertha. He knew she would wash them and give them to the Salvation Army.

When he was done, he had two bags of bottles, a half a bag of garbage and seven pieces of clothing. "Wouldn't people notice? Apparently not," he said. Again, he was met by Officer Murphy who said, "I told you it was a big party."

"It sure was, Mr. Murphy."

"You can put the garbage in the trunk. I'll drop it off at the Highway Garage. You have some things for Bertha too?"

"I sure do. She'll be happy," he said as he sat down.

"OK, here you are Scotty," as he pulled up to the Recycling Center. He pulled the bags of bottles out of the patrol car and said, "Thank you Mr. Murphy for the rides."

Officer Murphy said, "Have a good evening Scotty, thank you again," and drove off.

Scotty went inside. He was happy to see Mr. Jones who, along with Bertha, were like family to him. He couldn't remember how long he'd been doing this, but it was almost twenty years. Before that, he'd been in one of those places for people who couldn't help themselves for many years. Then one day he was put here and given this job. A man with gray hair from the university taught him how to do what he does today. He couldn't remember his name. Come to think of it, he hadn't seen that man in a while. Mr. Jones sorted through the cans and bottles for him. Even gave him a room when it got too cold for his tent and lean-to. Mr. Jones allowed him to shower and keep his things there too. Bertha washed his clothes and left them here with his favorite sandwiches, peanut butter and jelly. He had it pretty good.

He thanked Mr. Jones and went to his room. There were his clean clothes, peanut butter and jelly sandwiches and some chocolate chip cookies. He waited to eat until he showered and dressed. This was his favorite time of the day. Being clean. There was some coleslaw there too which brought out a big smile. He didn't care for those cold salads with potatoes or macaroni. He wasn't sure how to tell Bertha that, so he fed the chipmunks and birds with those when he got back to his tent in the morning. He used to let the chipmunks crawl all over him but not anymore. One of them bit him on the chest when a piece of macaroni fell on him. Even he knew the difference between skin and food. That really hurt.

If there was some macaroni left, he would walk down to the river and feed the fish. He had several that would take it right out of his hand. He enjoyed this. What he couldn't understand was where they went. Where did they come from? He wanted to join them, but he was afraid of the water. Often, he would watch them for hours as they would come to the edge of the shore to beg. He would finally give them the last pieces and go back to his tent. Sometimes he would read his comic books or go over to the boulders at the end of the island to listen to the music the old people played at the old people's home. Most of the time the music sounded so different than what he heard from people driving around. He could actually understand what they were saying. Those were the good mornings when the weather was nice.

There were times when there were people playing shows with just talking. He didn't like those. He went over by the college those days. He didn't like their music as much, but those talking shows he didn't understand. What do people get from talking when they try and talk over each other? Don't need it, too many other things to do.

The sun was starting to touch the trees. He needed to get ready to go out. Soon the leaves will be letting in more light. The college students would be back, and they'd start kicking that round ball around. The man who taught him his job liked that game. He told Scotty about it.

He wished he could run and kick like that. It wasn't that he didn't try. He did, but that ball—well, it was fun to watch. Lately though, he was having trouble walking very far. Just like the man with the gray hair before he left. "Did that mean his hair was gray?" He'd go by that store with dresses tonight and see. Was that why Mr. Jones had him see that Doctor? He was nice. He talked to him like he knew him. Scotty remembered when the Doctor asked who it was that could sign for him. He told the Doctor, "I can." He took up a pen and wrote Scotty. "See."

The Doctor said, "Yes. I'll check with Mr. Jones." Scotty didn't know why since he had showed him, he could sign. He wants to see Scotty again. "That's OK," he told the Doctor. "You can come to see me any time, except when it's cold."

He adjusted the handkerchief somebody with one of those motorcycles gave him to wear. It helped keep hair out of his eyes. That must be why the rider had one on. He would have to find his shoes so he could get his hair cut. Miss Lois always made him wear shoes where she worked, even though it wasn't cold. The Doctor was the only other one who had him do that. Mr. Jones told him that before they went.

Scotty forgot to look before rounding the tree and headed down the hill. He stopped when he saw three girls without clothes on. He turned and walked back around the tree. One of them smiled at him, but he didn't think the other two had seen him. Was that one dark skinned? He peeked back around the tree. She was, but she looked just like the others, so he walked back to the road. Why did they like to have no clothes on? He didn't know. He had never done that, although he had thought about it. But not when it was still light out. Was it because they washed them in the river? Seemed like too much work. Maybe that's why there were extra clothes: they just forgot what they had.

He got to the park. He found a bench to rest. He watched some kids playing tag and wanted to join in but was too tired. When he got up, he walked by the dress store. If he had gray hair, he'd have to train someone to take his place. He wasn't sure who, but he knew that would be his job. But then, where would he go? He wouldn't have anything to do. Maybe he would see the man who trained him. He hoped so. He had enjoyed his job and would tell the man so. He would have to ask Mr. Jones tonight.

He got up, checked the containers marked "Scotty" for bottles and cans. There were only a few. By the time he got to the corner, the light had changed so he had to wait. Somebody yelled "retard" as they drove by. He looked around but didn't see who they were talking too.

He crossed the street and went directly to the dress shop. He had to squat down to look in the mirror. His hair was gray. Oh no, that was why he was short of breath and felt lazy. Was he now going to have to go to that old people's home? He was about to get up when he heard, "Scotty, are you alright?"

He turned around to see Officer Murphy. "Yes," he said.

"What are you doing?" Officer Murphy asked.

"I'm just checking to see if my hair is gray," he said.

"Your hair has been gray for a while now," Officer Murphy replied.

"It has? Why hasn't anybody told me?" Scotty questioned.

"I didn't know that was important to you. Why is that?" Officer Murphy asked.

"Why is what?" he asked.

"Why is it you want to know the color of your hair?" Officer Murphy asked.

"Because if it is gray, I need to train someone to do my job. That is what happened to me. That man at the university trained me to do his job, then he left. I don't know where to, but now I need to train someone just like he trained me," he said.

"Oh, now I see. Who is that going to be?" Officer Murphy asked.

"I don't know," Scotty said.

"Can you continue to do the job until we find someone?" Officer Murphy asked.

"Oh, yes. But I am getting tired easier. I know now it is because of my hair."

"Do you want a ride anywhere Scotty?" Officer Murphy asked.

He didn't feel so good so he said, "Recycling Center if you can, Mr. Murphy."

"Sure can, Scotty, hop in. I'll tell them at the office to keep an eye open about finding someone you can train," Officer Murphy said.

"Don't do it right away," he said while getting out of the car. "Thank you, Mr. Murphy," as the patrol car pulled away. Mr. Jones was off tonight, but Ben took the bag from him and asked, "Slow night tonight, Scotty?"

"Yes. I'm tired, Ben. See you later," he said and walked back to his room. Maybe he would feel better after a shower.

When he came out, he thought he'd feel better if he ate. He ate part of a sandwich, then lay down.

Bertha Connors found Scotty around noon. She notified the Police Department. Officer Murphy felt bad he didn't take

Scotty to the hospital when he had mentioned he didn't feel well.

Mr. Jones made the arrangements for the funeral. He bought a lot next to his in the cemetery with the town and college covering funeral expenses.

Scotty never asked nor did he know what happened to the money received from the bottles. That wasn't important to him. Shortly after Scotty started his job, a scholarship was set up at the university for a soccer player in need.

Over the years, it grew to a scholarship for a men's team player and a woman's team player. Scotty loved to watch them practice but never went to the games, there were too many people. If Scotty had, he would have known the names of the players who benefited from 'Scotty's Award' since they were listed in the game day programs. It was a way for everyone to know, a way of saying a public "Thank You."

25

༄

Alphabet

The telephone listing said the fabric store was located at 4 Main. We drove by it twice because we didn't see a business sign. Finally, I parked the car thinking it had to be one of the two old buildings across the street. The only visible signage was in a window. It read, "Yes, we're open."

That was enough for my wife. You would've thought it was an ice cream shop by the way she took off, leaving me and our granddaughter in the car. My wife didn't have a major decision to make like the one happening in the back seat. Do we bring in the floppy doll with the yellow dress or the rest of a cookie? Even at the age of two, food won out as she carefully cradled what was left of the cookie in her hand while I carried her across the street to the store.

My wife did look back our way just before entering the store. When we entered, she was already walking up and down the various aisles taking in the array of colors and patterns. Upon seeing her, our granddaughter excitedly said, "Grandma, there you are!"

"I didn't hide very well, did I?" she joked as she picked up our granddaughter and gave her a squeeze, causing her to laugh. "Can you show Grandpa all the pretty colors in the store?" she asked.

With a big smile that suddenly took on a look of importance she said, "yes." She walked up to me and grasped my small finger. With only a slight bit of hesitation, she started towards the other end of the store. Unsure where to start, we finally ended up in an aisle that had a double rack of fabric. The bottom was mainly solid colored material, but the top rack had animals on it. "Up, Grandpa," she pleaded. "Up!" I bent over and picked her up. By now her hands were empty. Her cookie was gone.

"Look, Grandpa, a dog." She proceeded to bark like a dog. Then started to meow like a cat. Then came a low moo for a cow. The monkey was next, but she didn't try to imitate it. She tried to act like she didn't hear me when I asked, "What sound does a monkey make?" She just said, "Look, Grandpa, a lion. Grroowwll." After almost every animal she saw she made the corresponding sounds. But there was one animal that left her confused. That was the seahorse. She couldn't understand how it could have the name of a horse, especially if it didn't have legs to run on. With that, it was time to move on.

My wife and the attendant were now going through mounds of fabric combinations in shared excitement. This was going to be a bedspread for our granddaughter's birthday, and it was going to be a surprise. After raising two boys, my wife was finally getting an opportunity to purchase things for girls. Her excitement showed. The array of colors and patterns assembled on the counter were endless but lacked the shades of blue that had graced our home. Shades of pink and lime green dominated the counter surface.

In this section of the store, there was also a table where our granddaughter saw several books. Reaching up for one she said, "Look Grandpa, book, can you read to me?" and handed it to me when I sat down. She loved being read to. "Up, I up, lap?" she asked. I said, "Yes," and picked her up and placed her on my lap.

It was a book for making a quilt of cartoon characters. She would name the character and what cartoon the character was from. I was surprised how many she knew. If she didn't know them, she would just turn the page.

After a while, she started to get tired of that. Fortunately, there was a children's book also on the table. I picked that one up and read it to her. It was about a little girl and her dog. It reminded her of her own dog, Samson or Sammy. She liked it so much that she asked me to read it again. When it was done, she asked to get down and started to walk on the floor like a dog. She barked as if to let me know that I was supposed to follow her. Up this aisle we went, then down the next. Fortunately, we were the only customers in the store at the time. Just when I thought she was getting tired of this game she would bark and turn down another aisle. During a moment of indecision, we heard someone say, "Too bad we couldn't find some material with the alphabet on it."

Her face lit up as she sprang to her feet and said, "Here, Grandpa." As we started toward an aisle we had walked down earlier, she stopped and grabbed at a fabric. "This one. This one, Grandpa," she repeated.

I bent over and picked it up. I had to put on my glasses since the letters were so small and sure enough, it did have the letters of the alphabet. How did she know that? I picked her up with the fabric and brought it up to the counter and asked. "Are you looking for material that has the alphabet on it?"

"Yes," the clerk said. "But we don't have... Where did you find that?"

26

∿

Wet Leaves

The day turned out better than what had been forecast. The wind ushered in by the cold front cleared the sky by late afternoon. He was now wishing he had taken the time to put on a windbreaker underneath his light jacket. The wind blowing the leaves around made it hard to hear sporadic movement.

The squirrels were making their last runs before sunset. The chickadees and robins would arrive soon to roost for the night. This was the time when the deer usually start moving.

The first sounds had started off to his front right. They were louder than normal for a deer, which got his attention. This being early in muzzleloader season meant you could also encounter bear, since they hadn't hibernated yet.

Brief sounds came from almost in front of him. His body was starting to cramp up, but he didn't dare move to avoid detection.

With the loss of light, the wind was dying down now. The chickadees fluttered through, then came the robins. What sounds he thought were made by deer were off to his left, but still cautiously coming towards him.

The first sight of a leg moving through a break in the vegetation sent his heart pounding. How many years had it been? It was still exciting. Then another one moved, but their bodies were still hidden. They were too far off for a safe shot. It will be dark by the time they get close enough.

He looked around to see where he could find cover for tomorrow so he could get closer to where they were bedding down. When he looked back, they were walking away from him purposefully. He had barely moved, what happened? It was now time for him to leave since they weren't coming this way and before his position was compromised. As he got up, he made sure to walk on the pine needles so there was less chance of his movements being heard. He worked his way straight back away from where he saw the deer traveling.

Then he remembered the sounds that were unusual and froze. He was moving right towards where he last heard them. Taking everything in, he spent a lot of time looking into the trees and a blow down off to his right. He quietly moved away until he noticed a smell that was not natural to the woods.

Slowly he walked up to a large pine tree on top of a small ridge and peeked over. There was a hunter leaning on a log with his pants down. Now it was clear why the deer turned away.

Not sure what to do, he decided to let the hunter know he was there rather than take a chance of getting shot in the fading light. "I didn't know anyone was back here," he said, startling the hunter.

As the hunter looked his way, he said, "I'll wait over the ridge until you're finished."

"Thank you," the other hunter said. "Damn Bill's cooking. He thinks everybody should like hot and spicy foods, which taste good, but oh do you pay for it later." There was a pause before he asked, "Do you have any toilet paper with you?"

"No, but you're in luck. The leaves are wet and fresh off the trees," he offered while moving further away.

"That's true," the man muttered, then mumbled something else he didn't understand.

A short time later the other hunter finally came over the slight ridge and said, "I'm Rick."

"And I'm Adam. If you would've been much longer, we would have needed flashlights to get out of here," he added, joking.

"I don't really know this area so I'm glad you came along," Rick said as they picked up their pace.

Finally, Rick asked, "Did you see anything? I didn't."

"No, I didn't either," Adam replied, which wasn't really true, as they walked on in silence. They finally came through a small cut when Adam said, "The main road is that way," pointing off to his right.

"Thanks," Rick replied. "I thought you were lost and was just about to tell you so. Nice mixture of hardwoods and pines, but you can't eat scenery. He walked down the logging trail without saying another word. He didn't ask where Adam was going for the night, even though his camp was just over the ridge.

27

❧

The Stoplight

As I pull up to the stoplight from my house, it starts to sprinkle. A young woman standing at the corner puts her thumb up and walks toward my vehicle. I roll down the window, but she gets into the car without saying a word. As she buckles up her seatbelt she asks, "Are you going to Burlington?"

Surprised, I say, "Yes, but why are you in my car?"

"I'm going to be late for a meeting and the bus is behind schedule," she says.

As the light changes, I ask, "When is your meeting?"

"At nine o'clock. I know I'm late, but I already called them." A quick look at the clock shows it's after ten thirty. "Did you know it was going to rain today?" she asks.

"No." I say as I stop for the light, but she is already saying something about being raised on a farm. "Yep, I have always worked. Working now, but my rent takes most of what I make. Used to work thirty hours but they cut everyone back to twenty hours to give more people a chance to work. Isn't that nice?" she asks sarcastically.

I nod, but she doesn't notice as she is now talking about being homeless. "Did you know they don't allow candy in the shelter? What kind of car is this anyway? Well, I didn't either. This is a nice ride. Don't get me wrong, I've always worked my whole life," as we stop at yet another stoplight.

"I work at a restaurant, but the patrons like to look at my chest," she says, turning slightly towards me and putting her shoulders back. I notice her actions out of the corner of my eye. If I were in the curbside lane, I would have pulled into a driveway to let her out, meeting or no meeting.

"Did you know it was supposed to rain today?" she asks again as she settles back into the seat. "I didn't either. I'm applying for the manager's position at the restaurant. I know I can do it. I'll make those guys pull up their pants or roll their pant legs up, so they don't drag on the floor," she says and burst out laughing slapping the dash of the car as she does.

Why didn't I lock the doors when I started out this morning? We haven't made a light the whole way. We still have at least five blocks to go. What in the hell is this woman on?

"Did I tell you I work in a restaurant? Some of the workers left when we got our hours cut. They felt the company didn't want to pay for our health insurance, but I'm not sure. It doesn't matter. I wouldn't pay for anything anyway. What day --- wow, why did that college kid just step out in front of us? They didn't even look. Must be on mom and dad's--- whoa, that one hasn't looked up from her phone once. Must be watching a hot video," she says as she turns in the seat to try and see as the young woman walks by.

"When we get close to where you want to get out, let me know so I can pull over." If she doesn't tell me, I'm not that far from the police station now.

Finally, she says, "Ok. The next block will be fine. I'm going to apply for disability even though I'm just thirty. The tough life I've been living has just been too much on my body. I may look older, but I'm just thirty."

I'm stopped, sitting along the side of the road at the corner where she wanted to get out. Suddenly she realizes we aren't moving and there is no light. She opens the door and says, "I decided, I'm going to apply for the manager's job." She doesn't even look to see if someone is coming, but just gets out and walks away.

Suddenly I hear "Stairway to Heaven" on the radio as I lock the doors. I wait until traffic clears before pulling out. At the light I said aloud, "Did that really just happen?"

About the Author

Roger Watters' prior books are of poetry which was a form he became comfortable with when he came back from Vietnam. They are: *From the Avenues of the Mind, Toothpick Forest, Stationary Witness, Who Stayed*, and *Voice of My Pen*.

He was asked to do a book on the history of Diamond Sportsmen's Club. This club was formed after the land became available as a result of court action. The club that had leased the land, decided not to try and purchase the property. That was when several members decided to try and form a club and buy the property, Roger was one of them. As a result, *Diamond Faces - The Story of Diamond Sportmen's Club* is available through the club.

CPSIA information can be obtained
at www.ICGtesting.com
Printed in the USA
FSHW010059040122
87362FS

9 781949 066975